Where's Stephanie?

Where's Stephanie?

A Story of Love, Faith, and Courage

Based on a True Story by

Lenora Livingston

Second edition, May, 2015
Library of Congress Control Number: 2014917740
CreateSpace Independent Publishing Platform
North Charleston, South Carolina
ISBN-10:1511737417
ISBN-13:9781511737418
Printed in the United States of America
Any people depicted in stock imagery provided by Thinkstock are models, and such images are being used for illustrative purposes only. Certain stock imagery © Thinkstock.

The names, details, and circumstances may have been changed to protect the privacy of those mentioned in this publication.

This is an autobiography. The stories and anecdotes in this volume are true accounts drawn from the author's life experiences and have been reconstructed as the author has remembered them, to the best of her ability. In some cases, for the sake of the narrative flow, she has created conversations and some scenes, and adjusted chronology. Some names, geographic locations and details have been changed to protect identities.

I dedicate this book to my best friend,

My number one critic,

And the love of my life,

My wonderful husband, Werner.

And

To the memory of my writing coach

Mark Weston, Playwright

Who passed away before he could
Receive an autographed copy of
My first edition.

THE STARFISH STORY

As an old man was walking along a
shoreline littered with starfish,

He saw a young girl gently tossing
the starfish back into the sea.

"Why are you doing that?"
he asked the young girl.

The old man told her she
was wasting her time,

There were thousands of starfish
washed on the shore,

Saving a few starfish won't
make a difference.

As she picked up another one and
gently tossed it into the sea,

She said, "I made a difference
to that one."

My Acknowledgements

I CANNOT FIND enough words to thank my editor, my fantastic husband, Werner, enough. His many hours of marking my typos and sharing his ideas for improvement have made a huge difference in the final outcome of this book. Most important, he didn't kill me during the process, because I know I had to be extremely difficult to live with.

I will be forever grateful for Mark Weston's writing classes. His encouragement to write with feelings has not only helped me immensely when writing *Where's Stephanie*, but has also proved to be very therapeutic to me.

I will be forever grateful for my friend Suzanne, a woman of true faith. If I never believed in divine intervention before, I do now. She was put in my life for a much bigger reason than I could have ever dreamed of.

Where's Stephanie exists because of the support and encouragement of the following people. Through one way or another, they have all contributed to the final outcome of this book: Andrea, Cadra, Cathy, Debbi, Linda, Lorraine, Louise, Martha, Mary Ann and Russell.

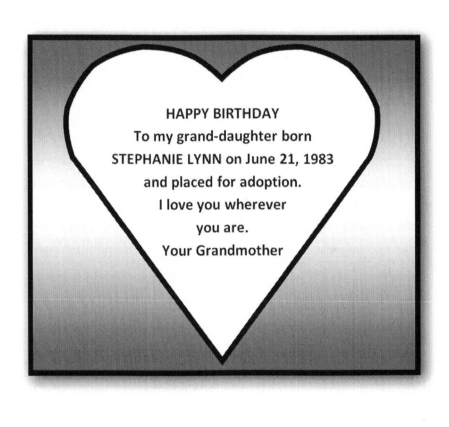

HAPPY BIRTHDAY
To my grand-daughter born
STEPHANIE LYNN on June 21, 1983
and placed for adoption.
I love you wherever
you are.
Your Grandmother

Where's Stephanie is based on a true story written from personal experience, interviews, and from documents obtained from the South Carolina Department of Social Services. Names of people, businesses, and geographical locations have been changed and, for the sake of narrative flow, conversations and some scenes were created to more accurately depict the story. The author was in New York City right before 911, and the walking up Broadway scene did happen exactly as written, but not the day before 9/11.

At the end of this book there is information on Adoption Searches, that is designed to help people who would like to locate someone they have been separated from by adoption.

CHAPTER 1

— ✦ —

The Ultimate Sacrifice

IN 1982, ON a brisk afternoon in early December, a 1973 Cougar pulled into the driveway of a middle-in-come, ranch-style suburban home near Greenville, South Carolina. The well-maintained home was nestled among dogwoods and towering pines. At the corners of the house, an abundance of pink sasanquas had already emerged from their buds for the season, and a large bed of freshly planted and mulched golden chrysanthemums embraced both sides of the front steps.

Twenty-two-year-old, handsome, lean, and athletic Ian McKinney hopped out of the car and walked toward the front door. He was greeted with a big hug from his mother, Anna Weber, and her faithful dog, Leighroi. Anna, a tall, attractive, middle-school, social studies teacher, was in her early forties. Ian was her oldest son. Her other son, Martin, was attending college on a baseball scholarship in a different part of the state.

Ian joined his mother in the kitchen part of her great room, where she poured them both a tall glass of iced tea and then handed Ian his. He sipped, saying, "Mom, you sure make the best iced tea."

"Thanks," she responded with a smile. "You always say that." Sensing something was wrong, she asked, "Now, what brings you here? You live too far away to just drop by."

"I have a problem," he said hesitantly.

What could be that bad, Anna wondered. Just two weeks earlier Ian and Shari Adams had announced their engagement. Shari was a lovely, young woman, who definitely met Anna's seal of approval. She asked him, "Is everything okay with you and Shari?"

"Yes, Shari and I couldn't be any happier," Ian responded. Then taking a deep breath and shrugging his shoulders, he said, "Mom, I just don't know how to start."

Anna calmly told him, "Then, just spit it out."

Ian took another deep breath and confided, "Something happened that shouldn't have, and a girl I dated this past summer is pregnant."

Anna was totally unprepared for this. She quietly digested Ian's words. The seriousness of the situation was overwhelming. The excitement of the past two weeks with joyful visions of Ian's upcoming wedding had just collided with her fears of what might happen to her first grandchild.

"Mom, I'm sorry. Maybe I shouldn't have told you about this," Ian said apologetically.

"No, I'm glad you did," Anna reassured him, while still trying to collect her thoughts. "Who's the young woman?"

"Tara Harper," Ian responded. "You taught her when she was in middle school."

"Tara Harper! I remember her well. She was a good student, a beautiful and delightful girl." Then as Anna started to relax, she added "I wish I could be happy about this. Hearing that I'm going to be a grandmother for the first time should be a joyful occasion. There's been a huge void in my life since your sister Wendy died. But having a baby around, a new life…"

Ian explained, "Mom, I really loved Tara and I still love her, but I don't love her the way I love Shari.

"Ian, I'm not concerned about what caused your problem. I'm concerned about what to do about it," Anna stated firmly. "What are your options? Can you get Shari to put off your wedding long enough for you to marry Tara so she can keep your baby, don't consummate your marriage, then get an annulment and marry Shari?"

"Mom, I can't tell Shari I've gotten another woman pregnant!" Ian stated firmly.

Fearful that if Ian didn't marry Tara, her grandchild could either be aborted or placed for adoption, Anna retorted, "But you can't leave Tara in the lurch!"

She explained to Ian his options. Abortion was out of the question. She was highly opposed to the use of abortion as a form of birth control. Having a child out of wedlock was absolutely scandalous. If he didn't marry Tara, he would put her in the position of raising an illegitimate child with all the stigmas attached. Both Tara and his child would be shunned and publicly ridiculed. That would negatively affect both Tara and their child for the rest of their lives. When it came to adoption, she knew there was an extreme shortage of adoptable babies ever since the Supreme Court's decision of Roe V. Wade legalized abortion. There were a lot of good families who would love to adopt Ian's baby. She boldly told Ian, "Adoption is an option, but this is our flesh and blood we're talking about. I want this baby to be a part of our lives!"

"I don't know what to do," Ian responded, feeling worse than he had before their conversation began.

Knowing that the final decision would be Ian's, Anna calmly advised him, "You have to do what's best for all concerned, including the baby. Whatever decision you make now, has to be something you can live with the rest of your life."

After a week or so had passed, Anna assumed no news was good news. But her complacency was interrupted one night by a phone call from a friend, who told her that Ian had visited him earlier in the day asking to borrow money for an abortion. Anna was extremely relieved when her friend told her that he did not give Ian the money.

She immediately called Ian and angrily told him, "Gene just called and said you tried to borrow money from him for an abortion."

"Yeah, but he didn't give it to me," Ian said defensively.

"Does that mean Tara's not going to have an abortion? Or did you get the money from somewhere else?" she asked.

He responded, "She's still having the abortion. I don't know where she got the money for it, but it wasn't from me."

"That's not the point!" Anna demanded, "You've got to stop the abortion!"

"I can't. Tara's terrified that her parents might find out she's pregnant," he argued.

"I've already lost my daughter and I don't want to lose my grandchild too!" Anna said. She thought about telling him about the miscarriage she had had after his sister died, but that was one quiet pain she would continue to keep to herself.

Ian told her it was too late to stop the abortion, that Tara was scheduled for the first appointment when the doctor's office opened at ten o'clock the next morning. Anna reminded him that he would have to live with whatever decision he made for the rest of his life.

She hoped he would find out what it would take to stop the abortion and then do so, but deep down she feared that he wouldn't.

She told her husband, Richard, about Ian trying to borrow money for the abortion and how she wanted to try to stop it. He quietly told her that he didn't think that was a good idea. Anna firmly responded, "This is my grandchild we're talking about! If I don't at least try to stop it from being aborted, it'll haunt me for the rest of my life."

The next morning, shortly before ten o'clock, a very attractive eighteen-year-old Tara Harper was in the waiting room of Dr. Brantley Holcomb. Another young woman was seated beside her. Tara filled out an abortion consent form and gave it to the receptionist who was seated behind a window. She sat back down, and while waiting to be seen by Dr. Holcomb, she drifted into thought.

She remembered the night that she and Ian had dinner together at his apartment. He impressed her by preparing the most awesome spaghetti she had ever eaten. He told her that his mother told him that if he and his brother learned how to cook, their future wives would appreciate it. So she taught them how to make spaghetti, but unfortunately, that was the only thing she had taught them how to cook. Tara's contribution to the dinner was a tossed salad with ranch dressing and garlic bread. Opening that second bottle of Chianti probably wasn't the best idea, but it was really good. She was lost in the moment, the solitude, the candlelit meal, the wine and Ian's kisses. Oh, how she craved his kisses.

The distant voice of a nurse calling her name brought her back to reality. "Miss Harper, Tara Harper, the doctor will see you now." Tara touched the hand of the young woman seated next to her, slowly got up, and went through the door being held open by a nurse.

At the same time across the Saluda River, Anna was at work instructing her seventh-grade, social studies students to pack their books in anticipation of the ten o'clock bell indicating morning break and the change of classes.

When the bell rang she walked hurriedly through the crowded halls to a closet near the teachers' work room. The closet was used as a phone room for teachers to make calls. There was a sign on the closed closet door that read "PHONE CLOSET-Please make calls brief."

Anna knocked on the door and heard a voice say, "Wait a minute." She waited anxiously. A couple other teachers needing to make calls started a line behind her. She impatiently knocked again. Finally, a teacher emerged from the phone room, scowling at Anna. Anna entered the phone closet, closed the door behind her, and dialed the number of her gynecologist. A receptionist answered.

Anna responded, "Hello, this is Anna Weber. I'm a patient of Dr. Stanford. Would you please tell me where in this city a girl would go for an abortion? My grand-child is scheduled to be aborted this morning, and I want to try to stop it."

The receptionist told her there was only one doctor in the Greenville area who performed abortions, Dr. Brantley Holcomb. Anna immediately associated the name with something negative she had heard on the evening news, but she couldn't remember in what context. She later remembered that, about ten years earlier, he had been charged with rape in one case and with murder for a late-term, third-trimester abortion in another case.

Anna asked for his phone number, and after the receptionist gave it to her, she wished Anna "good luck."

Anna thanked her, hung up, and nervously started dialing the number. She messed up and had to start dialing all over again. A glance at a clock on the wall read 10:07.

A receptionist answered, "Dr. Holcomb's office. Will you hold please?"

Anna, begged, "No, please don't put me on hold..." as she heard a click on the phone. She could do nothing but wait anxiously for the receptionist to pick back up.

The school bell rang indicating the morning break was over, and it was time for teachers to be back in their classrooms. To Anna's relief, the receptionist finally answered, saying "I'm sorry to have put you on hold. May I help you?"

Knowing that it was wrong to lie, but feeling confident that God would understand in this situation, Anna answered, "Yes, my daughter, Tara Harper, is scheduled to have an abortion this morning, and I don't want her to have it. I want her to have the baby."

The receptionist argued, "You can't stop her from having an abortion. She's of legal age." Anna knew she couldn't dispute that. Then the receptionist added, "And she's less than twelve weeks pregnant. It's your daughter's choice and legally you have no say so in the matter."

Anna didn't know where her next lie came from. It must have been divine intervention, because she found herself saying, "I'll have you know Tara is more than twelve weeks pregnant. I know because we were on the same schedule with our menstrual cycles. She's at least thirteen weeks pregnant."

The receptionist told Anna it was too late, that Tara was already sedated. Anna went ballistic, declaring, "It can't be too late! Tell Dr. Holcomb if he kills my grandchild, he will never hear the end of it, I'll have him arrested for murder!" Then, with the thought that maybe she should threaten to hit him where it might hurt him the most, in his wallet, she snarled, "I'll sue him for every dime he's worth!" Then she tearfully begged, "Please, don't let him kill my grandchild!"

The receptionist stated firmly, "Mrs. Harper, it's too late!" as she hung up the phone. Anna returned to her classroom full of students who teased her about being tardy without a late pass. Anna greeted them with a heavy heart, camouflaged with a big smile as if everything was alright.

Tara Harper's sister Nicole was only nineteen months younger than she was. They were always more like best friends than sisters. When Nicole came home from school earlier, she found Tara in a very bad state of mind. Tara confided that she had gone for an abortion earlier in the day, but somehow their mother had found out and called the doctor to stop it. Tara was terrified of what was in store for her when their parents got home from work. Nicole did the best she could to comfort her sister, but Tara withdrew to their shared bedroom and shut the door.

Later that day, Nicole was doing her homework in the kitchen, when their mother Andrea Harper arrived home from her job as a clerk-typist and started putting away several bags of groceries. Nicole watched her in total disbelief. She assumed her mother knew about Tara's visit to the abortion doctor. How could her mother so nonchalantly put away groceries when Tara was at the depths of despair? Why didn't her mother check on Tara's well-being?

Andrea asked, "Nicole, how was school today?"

Nicole didn't respond. She didn't understand how her mother could calmly ask how school was.

"Nicole? Didn't you hear me?" Andrea asked louder?

"Yeah!" Nicole responded angrily.

Concerned, Andrea asked, "What's wrong?"

"You know good and well what's wrong," snapped Nicole. "Why aren't you the least bit concerned about Tara?"

With that remark, Andrea instantly knew something was very wrong and went to her daughters' bedroom. She knocked on the door and called "Tara," but Tara didn't answer. She knocked again calling "Tara," but there was still no answer. "I'm coming in!"

Andrea opened the door and found Tara curled up on the bed in a prenatal position, her nose red and eyes puffy. Upon seeing her mother, Tara burst into tears, "I'm sorry Mama. I didn't want to have an abortion. I didn't want to hurt you and Daddy. I didn't know what else to do. I'm sorry. I'm so ashamed."

Shocked, Andrea asked, "You had an abortion?"

Sobbing, Tara responded, "No, I was going to until you called Dr. Holcomb's office and told them to stop it."

Confused, Andrea asked, "What? What are you talking about? Who's Dr. Holcomb? I haven't called anybody to stop anything!"

Equally confused, Tara asked, "You didn't call Dr. Holcomb?"

"No, it wasn't me." Andrea responded, very annoyed," Who would want to pretend they were me? I certainly don't like the idea of you being pregnant, but I'm glad you didn't have the abortion." Andrea proceeded to tell Tara that being pregnant was not the end of the world, that they would work it out, and that she wanted the baby.

That evening Anna received a phone call from Andrea Harper asking her if she was the woman who called Dr. Holcomb's office pretending to be her. Hesitantly, Anna responded, "Yes, it was me." She was not sure if Andrea would be angry with her for meddling in their business or of she would be grateful.

Andrea gratefully told her, "Thank you. I want this baby." The two expectant grandmothers continued a pleasant conversation, where Andrea invited Anna to a party for women only at their house the next weekend. Anna accepted the invitation. At the party Andrea pulled Anna aside where the two excited grandmothers-to-be quietly talked about how they were looking forward to sharing the joys of being grandparents together.

A few days later, Anna, Ian, Andrea, and Tara met in a mom and pop hamburger joint to discuss the baby's future. Andrea assured Ian and Tara, that if they marry, she and Tara's father would help them out financially until they got on their feet. Anna added that after bridal and baby showers, a lot of their immediate needs would be met. But Ian and Tara turned down their offers of assistance. They let their mothers know that they appreciated their thoughtfulness, but they wanted to decide for themselves what was best for their lives and futures.

Andrea agreed to abide by whatever decision Tara and Ian made. Anna hesitantly agreed, because in the back of her mind was the nagging fear that her grandchild would be put up for adoption.

Tara's father, Pete Harper, was a forty-year-old, easy-going, hardworking, and protective father of his two daughters. The evening that Andrea and Tara told Pete about Tara's pregnancy, they saw a side of him they never knew existed. But then Pete never had to deal with an unwed, pregnant, teenage daughter before.

"What do you mean Ian's mother pretended she was you and stopped the abortion!" he yelled. "What makes that meddling woman, what's her name, think she has the right to interfere in our affairs? That's none of her business! It's not her child that's going to cause her family shame by bringing an illegitimate child in this world. It's bad enough that her son got you pregnant. He can strut around like everything is just fine, while you carry the burden of his child."

In defense of her daughter's wishes Andrea begged, "Pete, calm down. Tara wants to keep her baby and I've told her I'll support her in whatever decision she makes. I was hoping you would be supportive too."

"Andrea, don't tell me to calm down," Pete demanded. "And Tara, let me get this straight. You're pregnant. Ian won't marry you. You don't have a job and you want to keep the baby. What has gotten into you? We didn't raise you to sleep around!"

"Daddy, I don't sleep around. It only happened once."

"One time!," he yelled. "You dated him all last summer and you expect me to believe you got pregnant after having sex only once? What do you take me for?"

Andrea reminded Pete that it only took them one time to get pregnant with Tara. Pete snarled at her, "That was different! And you're making things worse by planting ideas in Tara's head about keeping the baby. Okay Tara, you can keep your baby." He then added, "But not under this roof! You can keep your baby when you have the means to put a roof over your head, when you can pay for food, clothing and medical care for both you and your baby. Oh, you have to afford day care for the baby when you're working. And then there's the expense of transportation to and from work, plus insurance and the list goes on. You're eighteen with no job in sight. Good luck! I'm not paying for your mistakes!"

Andrea told Pete that he was being too harsh. She reminded him that they were just a couple of kids when they got married and had a baby right away. But Pete reminded her that Tara was not married. Andrea argued, "And that's more the reason we should help her."

Pete's final words to the situation were, "Okay, I'll talk to Ian. If I can convince him to marry Tara, I'll be more than happy to help them get off to a good start in life, but if he doesn't marry her, Tara's on her own if she keeps her baby."

The next morning, when Ian arrived at his job as a sales clerk at a sporting goods store in a strip mall, Pete was in the parking lot waiting for him. Pete demanded, "Ian, we need to talk."

"Mr. Harper, now is not a good time." Ian explained, "My boss is expecting me to open the store for him. Can you either meet me at lunch or see me when I get off of work at six?"

I'll be quick and to the point," Pete remarked, "If you don't marry Tara, she's going to have to leave town, live in a home for unwed mothers, and give her baby up for adoption. You don't have to stay married, just long enough so she can save face and keep her baby."

Ian asked Pete to let Tara decide what was best for her. Pete declared that he was letting Tara decide what was best for her.

With a glimmer of hope, Ian asked, "So, if she wants to keep the baby, then she can keep it?"

Pete snapped, "No, because if she decides that, then it's not what's best for her. By the way, how many times did you have sex with my daughter?"

Ian responded hesitantly, "Only once."

"Are you sure it was only once?" Pete questioned cynically.

"Yes, it was the only time," Ian stated firmly.

Then Pete demanded that Ian stop communicating with Tara. But Ian reminded him that the baby was half his, and he and Tara needed to communicate about the future of their baby. Quite angered by Ian standing firm in his commitment to communicate with Tara, Pete gave him one final ultimatum. "Tara wants her baby, but she can only keep it if she has a husband. You know Doug Barrow?"

Skeptically Ian answered, "Yes, why?"

Pete explained, "Doug said he would like to marry Tara, but only if she gives your baby up for adoption. So if you don't marry her, she can't keep her baby."

With a deep frustrated sigh, Ian responded, "I'm sorry, I can't marry her."

With that Pete declared, "Okay then, the baby will be put up for adoption and there's nothing you can do about it! I will never allow you to have the baby. You can mark my word on that!"

In a desperate attempt to keep his baby from being put up for adoption, Ian decided to tell his fiancée Shari about Tara's pregnancy. He told Shari that he loved her more than anything else and he hoped she would still love him after he told her what he had to say.

Shari's apprehensive response was, "Ian, you're scaring me."

He proceeded to tell her that he needed her to be understanding, that a girl he used to date was pregnant with his child. Shari immediately burst into tears. Then, when she realized that Tara got pregnant during the same time period when she and Ian were dating, she became hysterical.

"We weren't going steady then and I didn't realize how much I loved you until later and that's when I gave you your ring," he explained.

"That doesn't make me feel any better!" Shari cried.

"I was hoping you'd be understanding." Ian begged, "I don't want my baby to be placed for adoption. I know it's asking a lot, but can we postpone our wedding plans?"

That really freaked Shari out. Ian explained that he only wanted to postpone their wedding plans long enough for him to marry Tara, so she wouldn't have to put his baby up for adoption. He assured her that he and Tara would be married in name only until after the baby was born. Then they would get an annulment and he would marry her.

When Shari steadfastly refused his request to let him marry Tara until his child was born, Ian conceded, "Okay then, I won't marry Tara. I'll try to get custody of my baby."

The thought of that was more than Shari could handle. "And then what? You're not expecting me to raise another woman's child, are you?" Shari finally gave him an ultimatum, "Didn't you tell me a little while ago that you love me more than anything else in the world?"

"Yes," Ian responded.

Shari asked, "Do you want to marry me?"

"Yes, I do, more than anything," Ian answered sincerely.

"I won't marry you if you get custody of that baby!" Shari cried.

Tara left the comforts of home to spend the next few months at one of the many Florence Crittendon homes that serve unwed mothers across the nation. She chose the nearest one, which was over two hundred miles away in Charleston, South Carolina. Her parents told other family members, friends, and neighbors that she had gone away to school.

Anna imagined what Tara was going through, the loneliness she must have felt living so far away from home. Her heart went out to Tara. She wrote letters to comfort her and Tara wrote her back. In one letter Tara said she didn't understand why Ian wouldn't marry her. Although Anna never said so, she couldn't understand it either.

Months later, Ian was at the sales counter where he worked. The store had just opened and Ian was busily getting it ready for the day. Doug Barrow, Tara's suitor, a large strapping former university football player in his early twenties, approached the sales counter. He was shaking with anger. Ian's boss was in the background observing the confrontation.

Doug sneered, "You have a lot of nerve calling Tara!" Ian's boss glared at Ian and cleared his throat.

Ian, not wanting to jeopardize his job, asked Doug if they could speak outside. He assured Doug that he would join him in a few minutes. Reluctantly, Doug went outside, but glared through the window at Ian as he watched him prepare the cash register for the day. Ian took his time, hoping Doug would have time to calm down.

No longer being able to put off the inevitable, Ian joined Doug outside. "We can talk now, but we have to make it brief."

"If you contact Tara ever again, I'll rearrange your face to where no woman will ever look at you twice!" Doug threatened.

Ian, knowing he was outsized by Doug, knew he had to keep a cool head. He calmly said, "Well, you obviously don't know me very well. You don't know what I am capable of and I can hurt you too. I don't want that for either of us. You need to understand, whether you like it or not, Tara's baby is half mine. I need to communicate with her about the future of our child. So, don't worry. I'll not interfere with your relationship with her.

"That's the least of my concerns," Doug snorted.

"I understand you'll marry Tara only if she gives my baby up for adoption, and I find that upsetting," Ian said anxiously.

With a smirk on his face, Doug declared, "Why should I raise your kid, when Tara and I can have our own. If I'm going to be a daddy, I want to have the pleasure of making the baby."

Then Doug told Ian that when he refused to marry Tara, he gave up his rights to communicate with Tara and his rights to his baby. He threatened, "Tara's not keeping your baby and you can't do anything about it. So you stay out of her life for good or I'll personally see to it that you will regret it!"

When Anna's other son, Martin, came home from college for spring break, he found her crying. Baffled by why she would be crying in what was her favorite season of the year, he asked her what was wrong. She told him about Tara's pregnancy and the possibility of the baby being placed for adoption. Martin offered to marry Tara, but Tara declined.

On the evening of June 21, 1983, Andrea Harper called Anna to tell her that Tara had given birth to a baby girl. She assured her that both mother and daughter were doing fine.

The next day, Anna drove down to Charleston to meet her new granddaughter and to see Tara. She brought Tara a dozen red roses and a gift wrapped in white paper and a pink ribbon. When she arrived at Tara's room in the hospital, Andrea Harper greeted her and offered to take the roses and find a suitable vase. She left Anna to visit alone with her new granddaughter and Tara.

Tara had just finished feeding her baby and asked Anna if she wanted to hold her. Anna gave Tara the gift, and Tara gently handed Anna her new baby to hold.

The thrill of holding her baby granddaughter could only be compared to when Anna held her own first born child. Anna remembered how the fifteen hours of hard labor were instantly forgotten the moment after delivery when the doctor laid her daughter Wendy on her chest for her to embrace.

Tara's voice brought Anna back to the moment. She said, "I named her Stephanie Lynn."

"That's a beautiful name," Anna said proudly, remembering how she once thought that if she had been blessed with another daughter, that is the name she would have chosen. What a coincidence that this was the name chosen for her first grandchild.

Anna watched Tara open the gift that she had brought her. It was a tube of lotion. She told Tara, "I found that in a baby store. The clerk told me it's supposed to be good for eliminating stretch marks."

"Thank you so much. I can use that." Tara stated gratefully.

Having found a vase for the roses, Andrea brought them back in the room and placed them on a table near Tara's bed. Anna remembered that her camera was in her handbag that was still on her shoulder. Still holding baby

Stephanie and not wanting to put her down just yet, she twisted around where Andrea could see her handbag and asked, "Andrea, will you please take my camera out of my pocketbook? This occasion calls for taking pictures."

Andrea took the camera out of Anna's purse and the two grandmothers took turns taking pictures of each other holding baby Stephanie. Then Anna took several pictures of Stephanie by herself.

When it was time for Anna to leave for the long drive back home, she told Tara and Stephanie good-bye first. When she told Andrea good-bye, in a low voice Andrea said, "I'll let you know if Tara decides to keep her or put her up for adoption. It will be her choice."

Anna smiled and responded confidently, "She'll keep her." After seeing Tara holding and feeding Stephanie, she couldn't imagine her ever giving Stephanie up for adoption. But in the back of her mind she knew that adoption was a possibility that she hoped she would never have to face.

The next morning at the hospital, a tearful Andrea held baby Stephanie close, while Tara talked to a Department of Social Services caseworker from Columbia. Caseworker Taylor assured her that she was making the right choice by releasing her child for adoption. The caseworker left Tara and Andrea alone to say good-bye to Stephanie.

Andrea handed Stephanie to Tara. While holding Stephanie close, Tara whispered a prayer and added, "Please, God, watch over my baby girl. Don't let this be the last time that I see my little angel." She kissed baby Stephanie on the face and told her, "I'll always love you," as she handed Stephanie to a nurse who had been waiting outside the door.

Thirty minutes later, Tara and her mother returned to the Florence Crittendon office to meet with Caseworker Taylor and a Notary Public. Tara bravely signed the form releasing Stephanie for adoption. Then the Notary Public signed the document and affixed their seal. When they were finished, the caseworker handed Tara an envelope. She explained, "This is some information that might be helpful to you. It includes a list of counseling services that are available to you." She then asked Tara if she had any questions.

Tara told her, "I don't have any questions, but I have one request. Would you see to it that my daughter is placed in a religious home?"

Caseworker Taylor promised Tara that her baby would be placed in the best of hands.

That evening Andrea called Anna to tell her that Tara had made her decision and had signed papers releasing Stephanie for adoption. Anna was absolutely grief stricken. After having seen the love that Andrea and Tara showed for Stephanie, she couldn't understand how they could let her go. On the other hand, she could imagine how difficult it would be on Tara to be ostracized by friends and family for having an illegitimate child, not to mention the stigma Stephanie would have to endure.

Several days later, Anna called the Department of Social Services to ask about the possibility of her adopting Stephanie. She told them that, besides having her own children and being a school teacher, she had the experience of being a foster parent for the state of South Carolina and had kept ten children, one or two at a time, for a ten year period. She was told that grandparents have no rights when their grandchild is released for adoption. The only right she had legally was, she could place a letter in her granddaughter's file at Social Services, but the letter could not have any identifying information in it, no names of people or geographical locations. The mother's wish is what prevailed, and Tara had requested that her daughter be placed in a home away from the community where she lived.

A couple days later, a caseworker from the Greenville County Department of Social Services telephoned Ian to get him to sign the document releasing Stephanie for adoption. He drove to the small office manned by only one caseworker. Caseworker Harmon was cold, matter of fact, and controlling.

Upon entering the office, Ian said, "I'm Ian McKinney. You called me about thirty minutes ago, about signing a release form."

The caseworker looked over a document on her desk top and remarked, "Here it is. The baby's mother has already signed. All we need is your signature."

Ian apprehensively looked over the document, then said, "I don't understand the big rush."

The caseworker explained that the adoptive parents had already been cleared.

Ian argued, "But Stephanie is less than a week old. I was hoping you would reconsider letting me have custody of her."

The caseworker explained, "As I told you before, the mother wants her baby to be placed for adoption. We're legally obligated to honor the mother's wishes."

Ian pleaded, "But Stephanie is half mine."

In a condescending tone the caseworker told him, "You don't have the resources to care for a baby. You have a man living with you to help pay your rent."

Ian questioned, "Are you saying I don't have any rights?"

"You have the right to say either yes or no to signing this form," the caseworker snapped, "If you don't sign it, we'll have to take you to court and it could take years to be settled. Meanwhile, the child will have to stay in foster care. Sometimes these children get bounced around from home to home until the case is settled. Then she'd have to be uprooted to live with either an adoptive family or with you." Then in a threatening and haughty tone she added, "That is if the court grants you custody, which I seriously doubt it would."

Stunned, Ian responded, "I'm sorry. I can't sign it."

The caseworker retorted emphatically, "But you can't back out now. We already found her a family!"

Ian left the Social Services office to find a pay phone to call Tara. When he reached Tara, he found out that she had been crying non-stop since she kissed Stephanie good-bye.

He asked Tara if she was absolutely certain that placing Stephanie for adoption is what she really wanted. He told her that he knew she had already signed the document, but if she regretted it, he would not sign it. He insisted that they could still work something out. Tara reminded him that they could not afford a baby. He argued that people have babies all the time that they can't afford, but it works out. In a final plea, he reminded her that once he signed the document, Stephanie would be gone from their lives for good. Tara stood firm in her decision.

Defeated, Ian returned to the Social Services office and signed the document. It did not ease his pain in the slightest when the caseworker told him he was doing the right thing.

CHAPTER 2

A Living Gift

IN THE DENTIST office of Dr. Bryan Porter, in a rural town over two-hundred miles away from Greenville, Claire Ayers was assisting Dr. Porter who was working on a patient's teeth. Claire was the twenty-nine-year-old, attractive, energetic, and confident dental assistant to Dr. Porter. A phone rang in the main office. Another dental assistant, Patricia Adams stuck her head in the door and told Claire that a Department of Social Services caseworker named Lorraine was on the phone and wanted to talk to her.

Claire and her husband had filed for adoption several years earlier, and she assumed that the caseworker was just updating their file again. She told Patricia, "Tell her I'm busy and I'll call her back."

Patricia had a strong feeling that this call was extremely important. With urgency in her voice, Patricia told her, "No, you better answer it now!"

Dr. Porter urged Claire to take the call and added, "Patricia can take over here."

When Claire answered the phone, she was in for a surprise. The caseworker asked her what she would be doing Friday morning. Claire simply responded, "Working."

The caseworker told her, "We have a baby for you."

"You what?" exclaimed Claire excitedly.

Caseworker Lorraine repeated herself, "We have a baby for you. We want you to pick her up at the State Social Services office in Columbia Friday morning at ten o'clock.

Caught completely by surprise, Claire responded, "It's such short notice. This is Wednesday. "We don't have a crib yet."

"You don't need a crib," Lorraine responded. "Use a dresser drawer." Then she added, "It's unusual to get this much information on a baby. We have a lot of background information on both of the parents. You can't turn her down."

"Her? It's a girl?" Claire was ecstatic. "We're not about to turn her down. This is what we've wanted for years, a baby girl."

The caseworker suggested that Claire pick out a name for their baby and change it when they pick her up. The instant that Claire hung up the phone, she called her husband, Mike, at work and told him to get off from work Friday, because they needed to go to Columbia to pick up a baby. She was so excited that she hung up without telling him if it was a boy or girl. Mike called her right back and asked, "What are we going to have, a boy or girl?" He was delighted to find out that he was about to become the father of a baby girl.

Mike and Claire were both in their late twenties. They had been married ten years and tried everything in the book to get pregnant, including hormone therapy, but to no avail. When they filled out the initial paperwork to adopt, they said they would accept either a boy or a girl and even accept an older child, but they both really wanted a baby girl more than anything else.

On Friday, at the Social Services office in Columbia, Claire and Mike were left alone to read the background summary of the baby they were adopting, plus a Placement Agreement. The Social Services caseworker named Taylor joined them and asked if they had any questions. They had no questions, but said they felt most fortunate to be getting a baby with such a good background. When asked if they had picked out a name for their baby daughter, they smiled at each other and told the caseworker they picked out the name Sadie Leigh in the car on the way there.

Claire signed the Placement Agreement and handed it to Mike. Mike looked over the document, signed it, and asked the caseworker, "Does this mean we're foster parents?"

The caseworker corrected him, "No, it means you are the adoptive parents, and it needs to be formalized in a few months when the court changes her name to Sadie Leigh Ayers." She then invited the couple to accompany her to the Placement Room to meet their daughter.

When they entered the Placement Room, Caseworker Lorraine from their county was holding baby Sadie. She handed Sadie to Claire saying, "Here's your precious little daughter."

Mike asked, "How old is she? She's so tiny."

Caseworker Lorraine told him that his baby was only ten days old. She gave him a box, telling him there was enough formula to last until they got home. There were also diapers and other items of clothing in the box. Handing him a note she explained, "The foster mother sent this to you. It explains her formula and the care of her naval cord."

Caseworker Taylor told Claire and Mike that they would be receiving copies of the Placement Agreement that they signed after the commissioner signed them. She asked, "Do you need a copy now for the purpose of adding her to your insurance?"

Mike told her that all they needed to do was notify the insurance company about the adoption.

Caseworker Lorraine asked if they would need help with learning how to care for their baby. Claire laughed, saying they would need lots of help, but between her parents and grandparents, and Mike's parents they would have more than enough help.

Before Claire and Mike left, Caseworker Lorraine gave them an envelope, telling them, "This envelope contains a lot more background information than usual. Too often the mothers don't even know who the father of their child is, or they know very little about the biological father. It also includes non-identifiable background information of both of the biological parents. Plus, there are letters with non-identifiable information in them that the birth parents have written to your daughter."

In unison Claire and Mike said, "Thank you."

Caseworker Lorraine added, "We strongly recommend that, if you should give the contents of this envelope to your daughter, you wait until she is at least twenty-one years old. The records from this case will be sealed, but will be made available to your daughter, if she requests them, after she becomes twenty-one."

Mike and Claire thanked the caseworkers for everything they had done for them. Beaming with pride, Caseworker Taylor responded, "This is the part of our job we enjoy the most."

After Claire and Mike left with little Sadie Leigh, Caseworker Taylor asked, "Did you see how much Mrs. Ayers looks like the baby's biological mother? When she entered the Placement Room it almost left me speechless."

After Claire and Mike left the building and secured their new daughter in the car, Claire opened the envelope that Caseworker Lorraine had given them. She and Mike were curious about what was in the letters that the bio-logical parents placed in their daughter's file. They both cried while taking turns reading the letters, because they fully realized that Sadie's birth parents had made the ultimate sacrifice when they released their child for adoption.

When Claire and Mike returned to their small town, their first stop was at Mike's parent's feed and seed store. They entered the store with Mike carrying Sadie, "Ma, Pa, come meet your new granddaughter."

Pa asked, "How old is she? She's so tiny."

Claire answered, "Ten days."

"She's beautiful," smiled Ma, "What did you name her?"

Claire told her, "Sadie Leigh."

"She's so precious," then shaking her head in complete dismay, Ma asked, "How could someone give her away?"

Claire responded, "It wasn't easy for them. We feel very blessed to be chosen to be her parents. I hope we can live up to their expectations."

The next stop for the proud new parents was to Dr. Porter's dental office where Claire worked. Claire carried Sadie this time. They showed off their new daughter to Patricia, the dental assistant who answered the phone when Social Services called to tell Claire to pick up their baby. They also showed Sadie to Dr. Porter and to Martha. Martha was their minister's wife who also worked in the dental office. Having two adopted children herself, she was instrumental in persuading Claire to apply for adoption. She was always one of Claire's favorite people.

Their final stop for the day was their own home, a modest split-level home in a nearby tiny town with a population less than four hundred. Claire's grandparents, Mama and Papa, both in their seventies were waiting for them. They had been worried because Claire and Mike had been gone since early morning, but all concerns vanished the time they saw their new great-granddaughter. Papa immediately checked to see if Sadie had all of her fingers and toes.

The first thing of importance after they went in the house was to give Sadie a bath in the kitchen sink. Claire was all thumbs at first when handling her baby girl, but her grandmother helped out. When they were finished, Claire cuddled Sadie real close and told her, "You're all mine now, little Sadie Leigh. You're my adopted baby girl."

The caseworker had recommended that Claire and Mike, from the first day forward, refer to Sadie not just as their daughter, but as their adopted daughter. This was the first of many such occasions. They also started the tradition of celebrating Sadie's "Adoption Day" ten days after her birthday.

Claire's parents, who were in their fifties, dropped by to meet their new granddaughter as soon as they got off from work. Granddaddy and Grandmomma bonded instantly with the newest addition to their family, taking turns holding little Sadie for most of the evening.

Guests started arriving the first night and continued dropping by all hours of the day and night for over a week. During the first week, the new parents had over one hundred friends sign their guest register, not counting family members. Mike complained that he couldn't go to the bathroom without the door bell ringing.

Three days after they adopted Sadie, Claire took her to Dr. Schultz, a pediatrician in Charleston, an hour's drive from their home. Dr. Schultz gave Sadie a complete check-up. After he was finished he told Claire, "Your baby is just fine, but you aren't. Just sit down and calm down."

Claire told him, "I haven't had nine months to prepare for this. I didn't even have a crib when they called. They told me not to set up a nursery in advance, because the empty room would cause anxiety."

Dr. Schultz offered his best advice in a nutshell, "The first thing you need to know is she won't break. And second, there's only a few things that make a baby cry, being wet, hungry, tired, or sick. If she needs her diapers changed, change her. If she's hungry, feed her. If she's tired, soothe her to sleep. And if she's running a fever or if she's vomiting, not spitting up, but vomiting, call me."

Taking a deep breath, Claire responded, "You make it sound so simple."

Dr. Schultz assured her, "It is simple. But first you have to relax. You'll soon find that you will instinctively know what to do with her."

The next weekend, at Grandmomma and Granddaddy's modern ranch style home a baby shower was held. The home was packed with guests. The guest of honor was not the usual pregnant mother-to-be. The star of the show was little Sadie Leigh. During the three-hour shower, there was not one moment that Sadie was not being held. In this town with a population less than four hundred, the village would soon be playing a part in raising this very special little girl.

Several months later, Reverend Proctor officiated the Sacrament of Holy baptism in Sadie's Christening ceremony at a tiny Methodist church. There were only two rows of eight pews. The sponsors, in front of the congregation, were Claire, who was holding Sadie, Mike, Grandmomma, Granddaddy, Mama, Papa, Ma, and Pa.

Reverend Proctor first addressed the congregation, "Brothers and sisters in Christ, through the sacrament of Baptism we are initiated in Christ's holy church. We are incorporated into God's mighty acts of salvation and given new birth through water and the spirit. All this is God's gift, offered to us without price."

Reverend Proctor then spoke to Sadie's parents and grandparents, "Will you nurture Sadie in Christ's holy church, that by your teaching and example she may be guided to accept God's grace for herself to profess faith openly and to lead a Christian life?"

Claire, Mike and all the grandparents in unison promised, "I will."

The pastor put water from the chalice into the font. Claire handed Sadie to him. The pastor, holding Sadie in one arm, dipped his finger in the water and made a cross on Sadie's forehead and said, "Sadie, I baptize you in the name of the Father and of the Son, and of the Holy Spirit.

In unison all people in the church said, "Amen."

CHAPTER 3

Period Of Adjustment

WHEN HER INFANT granddaughter was placed for adoption, Anna felt alone in her grief. Losing Stephanie was like a death without a funeral, no flowers to cheer her up and no cards to console her. Richard wasn't any support. He expected her to "get over it." She couldn't turn to Ian for comfort. She blamed him for her sorrow. It would be a long time before she would realize that he was carrying his pain alone, too.

Several months later, in the Weber's master bedroom, an unhappy Anna was seated on the edge of her bed. She was dressed in formal attire for Ian's wedding. Wearing a suit and tie, Richard entered the room, checked his watch, and impatiently asked, "What are you doing? I thought you were ready to go."

"I don't want to go!" snapped Anna.

Confused, Richard told her, "You have to go. Ian is getting married in less than an hour. He's expecting you to be there."

"I don't care! I don't want to go," Anna repeated adamantly.

"But Ian is counting on you being there," Richard argued.

"How can he be getting married so soon after giving away his baby? Weddings are supposed to be for happy occasions," snapped Anna.

Firmly Richard told her, "You have to get over it! It's a done deal. Life moves on."

"I wish he'd married Tara," Anna responded weakly. "I don't have anything against Shari, but I wish he'd married Tara. I want my grand baby."

"Anna, get a grip," Richard demanded. "If you don't go to Ian's wedding you'll regret it. There's been enough pain already. Don't make it worse by not showing up for his wedding."

"I don't know if I can make it through the ceremony," Anna cried.

Richard told her again firmly, "Anna, you have to go!"

Giving in to reason Anna told him, "I'll go, but I'd rather take a beating."

"I'll be right there beside you," Richard said soothingly.

In a small Baptist church, Reverend Wilson was officiating in the wedding service for Ian and Shari. Anna and Richard were seated among the small number of guests.

To all of those in attendance Reverend Wilson said, "We are gathered together here in the sight of God to join together Shari Adams and Ian McKinney in holy matrimony. Should anyone here present know of any reason that this couple should not be joined in holy matrimony, speak now or forever hold your peace."

Anna tensed up. This was her opportunity to say what's been bothering her. "Shari, why didn't you let Ian marry Tara long enough to keep my grand baby from being given away? Ian, why should you be so happy when my grief is more than I can bear?"

Richard sensed Anna's feelings and squeezed her hand. She said nothing.

After the completion of their vows and the reception was held, Ian and Shari left for a Florida honeymoon, including visiting Disney World. Upon returning home they settled down in a small town outside of Greenville across the Saluda River from the university where Ian had attended. It was a quiet town bordering the river, where the city was laying out plans for the future Rivermont Park. It was the perfect setting for the young couple to settle down and start a family, an easy walking distance to the scenic river.

Anna realized that life was moving forward, maybe not in the way she wanted it to, but it was moving forward. It wasn't necessarily going to be easy, but she must move forward too.

A few weeks later, Richard was working in their rose garden when he observed Anna come out of their front door and walk to their mail box. He watched her as she took a deep breath, kissed an envelope, placed the envelope in the mail box, and put the flag up. She paused and then walked back toward their front porch.

With a most quizzical look, Richard asked her, "What was that all about?"

With the most cheerful attitude that he had not seen Anna display in months, she responded, "I've come to realize that the most important thing is that Stephanie is alive and, with that knowledge, I will always have the hope that one day I will be able to see her again."

Richard asked, "What does that have to do with the letter you just mailed."

Her confident response was, "I know the chances are slim and none that I'll ever see Stephanie again, but when I called the Department of Social Services a while back, they told me I could put a letter in her file. They said the letter could not have any identifiable information in it, no people names or geographical locations. Maybe by some miracle, when she grows up, she might ask to see her file."

Confused, Richard asked, "So, how's your letter going to help you see her again, if you can't put any identifiable information in it?"

Anna responded bluntly, "I put clues in it."

Richard echoed, "Put clues in it?"

"Do you have any better suggestions?" Anna asked. "I've done all I can. Now, all I can do is wait for a miracle."

Richard felt pleased to see that his wife was no longer in the slump that she had been in for the last few months.

CHAPTER 4

Early Years

SADIE WAS ADOPTED into a family with a strong religious background, rich in family traditions. She attended her first campmeeting when she was five months old. Her grandparents met there on a Tuesday night sixty years earlier and her mother first attended there when she was one month old.

Campmeeting is a non-denominational two-hundred-year-old tradition of families and friends getting together to celebrate and to thank God for the bounty of the harvest. Church services are held three times daily during the week-long event. It began in covered wagons, then in tents, and later in two-story wooden cabins which they call tents. The tents are deeded and passed down from one generation to the next. There are ninety-nine tents in a circle that is one-half mile around and a large tabernacle, open-air church, is in the center of the circle.

Campmeetings always mean great fellowship. Plus, the most fantastic crispy fried chicken one could imagine eating, grits with butter, butter beans, corn, and sweet iced tea are prepared on site. Mouth-watering deserts such as cakes, pies, cookies, and brownies are brought from the kitchens of those attending.

One of Sadie's earliest and fondest memories was of her granddaddy making "Hooey Sticks" at campmeeting. Hooeys were wooden sticks carved with notches and a propeller type pinwheel attached with a small tack to the end of the stick. When the notches were rubbed back and forth real fast with another stick, the propeller would spin in one direction, but when you yelled "Hooey" the propeller would change directions and spin the other way. How and why nobody knew, but it would do it every time. It was just a simple toy designed to entertain them. Sadie's granddaddy most likely learned how to make the "Hooey Sticks" from his father or grandfather.

Several years later, Claire and Mike divorced, but remained good friends. On Claire's shoestring budget, her father physically helped her build an adorable small home for her and Sadie. It was in the nearby town close to the dental office where Claire worked.

One afternoon in late spring, the framing was almost complete on a large play house that Mike, Granddaddy, and Pa were building for Sadie. Grandmomma was reading a magazine under a sycamore tree within earshot of the men. A picnic table was under a large live oak tree, a swing set with a sliding board was nearby, and a Norfolk Southern train track was across the street. Sadie was helping the men build the playhouse, as much as a four-year-old child could help. When she asked Granddaddy when it would be finished, he assured her that with her help it would be soon.

Then out of the blue, she asked him, "Granddaddy, did you know I was adopted?"

"Yes, I do, Honey. I remember the day your momma and daddy brought you home," her granddaddy responded affectionately.

"Momma said she and Daddy went in a room full of special babies and when they saw me, they pointed at me and said, 'We want that one,'" Sadie boasted proudly.

"That's because you were the most special of all the special babies there," he answered with a broad smile.

Pleased with her grandfather's affirmation, she responded, "That's what Momma said, too."

Claire came out of her house carrying a tray with a pitcher of lemonade, six glasses, and a plate full of cookies, as she declared it was time for them to take a break. Sadie, her father and grandparents joined Claire at the picnic table. Sadie took a few sips of lemonade, grabbed a cookie for each hand, and scurried off to her sliding board.

Claire commented to Mike that the building of the play house was a true labor of love and how much she appreciated him continuing to take an interest in Sadie's life after their divorce. Without hesitation Mike responded, "Why shouldn't I? She's my daughter. I'm enjoying every minute of it."

Claire, overwhelmed with joy, declared that she had no idea how full life could be until they got Sadie. Grandmomma described Sadie as a real jewel. Pa told them that having a child around again put a new purpose in his life. Their conversation was interrupted by a train whistle blaring in the distance, indicating a train would be passing by their home in a couple of minutes.

Granddaddy called to Sadie, and asked if she'd like to go wave at the train. Excitedly, she hopped down from the swing set and joined him. He picked her up and carried her across the street, so they could wave at the train as it went by their house.

When Sadie was in the second grade she wrote "Sadie loves Barrett" on her playhouse wall.

When Sadie was a little older, her granddaddy taught her how to throw a cast net to catch minnows to use as bait when fishing. He and Grandmomma, who was always by his side, also showed her how to put out trot lines to catch fish.

Sadie's kindergarten graduation was held in the fellowship hall of a Baptist Church in town. Sadie and her fourteen classmates were all dressed in fairy tale costumes. Among those in the audience were Claire, Mike, Granddaddy, Grandmomma, Mama, Papa, Ma and Pa. As one of the final performances of the graduation ceremony, her teacher, Mrs. Brazell, announced to the audience, "Sadie Leigh Ayers will now recite the 100th Psalm." Sadie, dressed as Cinderella, flawlessly recited:

"PSALM 100
Make a joyful noise unto the Lord, all ye lands. Serve the Lord with gladness; come before his presence with singing. Know ye that the Lord he is God: it is he that hath made us, and not we ourselves; we are his people, and the sheep of his pasture. Enter into his gates with thanksgiving, and into his courts with praise; be thankful unto him, and bless his name. For the Lord is good; his mercy is everlasting; and his truth endureth to all generations."

The next month at the Weber home, Anna was sitting at her desk with a mini-photo album in front of her. She was cutting a heart-shaped ad from the classified section of the newspaper. It read, "Happy Birthday to my granddaughter born Stephanie Lynn on June 21, 1983 and placed for adoption. I love you wherever you are. Grandma."

Anna opened the album. The first photo in the album was one she took of Stephanie when she was two days old. She flipped through several other photos taken of her holding Stephanie, of Andrea Harper holding Stephanie, and of Stephanie by herself. She skimmed by several other heart-shaped newspaper articles wishing Stephanie a Happy Birthday. She took out and unfolded a larger newspaper clipping. It was Tara Harper's and Doug Barrow's wedding announcement and photo. She read it, then refolded it, and returned it to its place in the album. Anna then inserted the heart-shaped article that she just clipped out of the newspaper into the album, placed the album in a desk drawer and closed it.

Ian, Shari, and their two-year-old son, John, traveled over one-hundred miles to spend the weekend with Shari's cousin Donnie Adams, his wife Patricia, and their four-year-old son, Joshua, at Lake Marion. Ian was carrying John as they walked down a slope to the Adams's pontoon boat which was tied to the dock. Ian told Donnie that this was the first time he and Shari had been boating since John was born.

Shari remarked, "I don't understand why we don't see more of each other, especially since you're my favorite cousin." Donnie agreed, stating that once you start a family, other activities tend to take a back burner.

Being impressed with the pontoon boat, Ian made the comment to Donnie, "I wish I had a new boat like this."

Donnie responded, "Actually, it's not new. It belonged to our best friends, but they got a divorce and wanted to sell it. They gave us an offer we couldn't refuse."

Ian, spotted the name SADIE LEIGH on the side of the boat and remarked, "That's a cool name for a boat."

Patricia told him that their friends named it after their little girl, Sadie Leigh, who they adopted around the same time Joshua was born.

When Ian told them that he had a daughter who was born around the same time as Joshua who was placed for adoption, Donnie's ears perked up. "What if our friends adopted your daughter?"

"No, she was supposed to be adopted in another part of the state," Ian responded with a heavy heart as Shari glared at him.

CHAPTER 5

Moving Forward

IN THE SAME small Methodist Church where Sadie was christened nine years earlier, her mother, Claire, married Dr. Bryan Porter in a small, sweet ceremony. She was wearing an off-white, ankle-length, Battenberg lace dress, and he was wearing a navy blue suit. Sadie and Bryan's eleven-year-old daughter, Adrienne, both wore aqua dresses trimmed with white lace. They played the double role of being both maids of honor and ring bearers. Claire's parents and grandpa were among the guests.

Reverend Proctor officiated. Reverend Proctor asked Claire, "Claire, what token do you give as a pledge of the sincerity of your love?"

Claire responded, "A ring."

Sadie handed her mother a ring.

Claire pledged to Bryan, "I, Claire, give you Bryan this ring as an eternal symbol of my love and commitment to you.

Claire placed the ring on Bryan's finger.

Reverend Proctor then asked, "Bryan, what token do you give as a pledge of the sincerity of your love?"

Bryan responded, "A ring."

Adrienne handed her father a ring.

Bryan pledged to Claire, "I, Bryan, give you Claire this ring as an eternal symbol of my love and commitment to you."

After Reverend Proctor finalized the service by pronouncing them husband and wife, wedding cake and wedding cookies were served along with punch. Sadie and Adrienne took their cake and punch to a pew in the back of the church. Half way through eating her cake, Adrienne took a sip of punch and asked, "Do you suppose your momma and my daddy are going to make a baby now? It would be kind of fun to have a real live baby to play with."

"It would be fun," Sadie responded, "but Momma can't have babies. That's why she adopted me. Somebody else had to make me, but she and Daddy were lucky enough to get me."

Adrienne asked curiously, "What's it like being adopted?"

"I don't know... kind of special. But, it's always like a little piece of me is missing. I don't know. It's like working on a jigsaw puzzle. You can almost see the whole picture, but some pieces are missing," Sadie answered quizzically.

Adrienne asked, "Do you ever wonder who your real mother is?"

"I know who my real mother is," Sadie snapped emphasizing the words real and is. "My momma is my real mother."

"I know that, but don't you ever wonder who gave birth to you?" questioned Adrienne.

"Yes, but they don't count, because they gave me away," Sadie grumbled.

"Don't you even wonder what they look like?" pushed Adrienne.

"Well yes, but, I don't want to talk about this anymore," Sadie said feeling uncomfortable.

"But aren't you curious?" Adrienne pushed further.

"I told you I don't want to talk about this anymore!" Sadie stated firmly.

At age nine, Sadie still liked to be the star of whatever was going on. The relaxed atmosphere at the small Methodist church gave parishioners the opportunity to perform in front of their friends and neighbors. One Sunday morning, in front of the fullest crowd that the tiny church would allow, Sadie and her ten-year-old cousin, Kevin, asked if they could sing "Lean on Me" to the congregation. Knowing that the two aspiring young stars had been practicing their routine for several weeks on their own, Reverend Proctor did not hesitate to include them in the program. While singing, they used body language to match the words of the song. They sang back to back when appropriate, gave each other a hug when the words of the song called for it, and made signs with fingers, like pointing to each other. They also sang God Bless America and, when they were finished, they received a standing ovation.

Several years later, when Anna and Richard were in their early fifties, they moved from Greenville to Summerville.

They didn't get to see their grandchildren as much as they would like, because of the hundreds of miles which separated them. Having four bedrooms and two sleeper sofas, their new home could accommodate large family reunions. Sometimes Ian's growing family would visit for weekends and holidays, and other times Anna and Richard were privileged to have their grandchildren visit one or two at a time, especially during summer break.

One particular weekend, Richard and Anna took Ian and his family for a boat ride to a small island via the Intracoastal Waterway. The island was totally uninhabited, with no restrooms, no stores, nothing but occasional wildlife. After their twenty-foot Renken was secured with an anchor out of the front of the boat to the land and another anchor out of the back of the boat into the water to keep the boat from washing ashore with the waves and tide, they settled in for some good family fun. Richard, Ian, and Shari and their two sons, John, age seven, and Miles, age four, were playing in the ocean. Anna was on the shore with her one-year-old granddaughter, McKenna, playing in the sand with the traditional little plastic bucket and shovel.

Suddenly, Miles screamed and ran out of the water. Everyone flocked around him as he cried non-stop while holding the calf of his leg. When Anna asked what was wrong, Ian explained that he was stung by a jelly fish.

Shari wanted to go back to the mainland, but Richard explained that it would take an hour to get there and Miles needed help right away. After everyone gave each other blank looks not knowing what to do to help the screaming Miles, Richard suggested, "Urine might help neutralize the jelly fish stingers."

Ian skeptically responded, "That's an old wives tale." But being open for anything that might help his wounded son, he added, "But it might be worth a try."

Anna held up the plastic bucket and asked, "Any volunteers?"

"John will do it," offered Ian.

In a negative tone, John asked, "Do what?"

Ian responded, "Pee in the bucket."

"Dad..." protested John.

"John," Ian ordered, "now's your chance to be a real hero to your little brother. Now, pee in the bucket."

Reluctantly, John took the bucket behind a bush, brought it back, and handed it to his father. Ian poured the contents on the calf of Miles's leg. Little did they know at the time what a lasting memory this would leave on all of them.

CHAPTER 6

Parallel Lives

ONE WARM SUMMER evening, Anna and Richard Weber, were relaxing on their front porch swing at their new home in an upscale subdivision in Summerville.

As Richard sipped his coffee, he sighed and said, "I'm really enjoying my new job, our new home, and living so close to the beach."

Anna agreed, "Me too, but the down side is we had to move so far away from our children and grandchildren."

Richard reminded her, "They're only a few hours away."

Anna took a deep breath and confessed, "Richard, I've been thinking about something for a long time. I'm not going to look for a job here."

Shocked, Richard asked, "What? Why? What will you do?" He was not prepared for her response.

"For the first time in my life, I want to try my luck at doing what I've always wanted to do since I was a little girl, but never had the confidence. I want to be a model."

"What? You have got to be kidding!" Richard argued, "You're not a spring chicken, you know. Besides that, you were making a good buck in the school system with all your years of experience and your certification beyond your Master's degree. What makes you think you can make it as a model?"

"I don't know that I can, but I have to try it." Anna stated her case, "I already have some basic experience from the little bit of local modeling that I did on the side when I was teaching school in Greenville. And last year, I got several call backs when I participated in The Millie Lewis Agency's modeling convention and one callback was from a New York talent agency. And remember last spring, when I was a winner in both the Dove Classic Model Search and the Leslie Fay Model Search? I entered those two contests on a lark, thinking there was no way I could possibly win either one of them, and ended up being a winner in both of them. That was from two different photographs taken by two different photographers. Well, that got me thinking that maybe I have what it takes. I don't know. All I do know is I have to try it."

"But that's such a big risk," Richard argued.

"I know, but there's a lot more to it than that," Anna added hesitantly. "I have never spent one night of my life away from home by myself. The thought was always terrifying to me.

"Remember, when I had all those flashbacks about being raped when I was a child? Prior to that, in order to live a normal life, I had completely blocked out what had happened to me. Watching Oprah Winfrey on TV helped trigger those flashbacks. One of her topics was the long term effects of being the victim of sex abuse, especially when it was never dealt with, which in my case it wasn't.

My mother was dead and I was afraid to tell my father, because the guy who raped me had a gun.

Richard said, "You should have told someone what happened."

"As an adult, I know that," Anna agreed. "But as a child I was frightened and confused. It wasn't until I watched Oprah and had those flashbacks that I realized how much that rape was still affecting my life.

"In my youth, I would wake up listening to Arthur Godfrey on the radio, describing the modeling scene in Miami's South Beach and Coconut Grove. My dream was to be a part of that one day. I knew without a doubt in my mind that I was born to be a model and I was supposed to be there one day doing that."

Richard interrupted, "You're not going to Miami! You saw how deplorable South Beach was when we rode through there on vacation several years ago."

"I know that and from what I've heard, the modeling scene down there has vanished. Now, please, let me finish. It's hard to talk about this," Anna pleaded.

"Watching Oprah Winfrey made me understand that when that reprobate raped me, he not only stole my virginity, he destroyed my confidence and he stole my dreams.

"I want to live the life that I have been afraid of living because of what happened to me. It will only be after I face my fears and follow those dreams, that I will be able to put that horrible chapter of my life completely behind me. It will be then, and only then, that I'll be able to consider myself a survivor instead of a victim."

Richard's only comment was, "I don't know how to respond to that."

Anna added, "The hardest part is I would have to commute to Atlanta."

"Atlanta! That's five hours from here!" Richard retorted.

"I know," Anna told him defensively, "I'll have to find a place to stay there during the week and come home on weekends. I talked to Susan, the owner of The Millie Lewis Agency, and she's going to arrange for me to meet the best agents there." She paused and then added, "Just the thought of me venturing alone to places I'm totally unfamiliar with frightens me more than I've ever been frightened in my life, and you know better than anyone, I've been through a lot. But I have to do it. I have to face my fears."

Richard acknowledged, "It sounds like your mind is already made up."

Anna agreed, "It is. I want you to know I'm not abandoning you. My decision has nothing to do with you. It's something I have to do. I know I'll always regret it if I don't at least try."

Richard conceded, "I don't want you to do it, but I won't stop you."

Partly saying thank you for not making it more difficult than what it already was for her, and partly to put Richard's mind at ease, Anna simply said, "Just remember I love you."

A couple weeks later, Anna loaded her twelve-year-old Toyota Tercel with a week's supply of clothes, toiletries, and cosmetics. She also packed headshots, which were eight by ten photographs of just her face with her resume on the back, and composite cards with multiple pictures of her on them, to give to Atlanta agents who would pass them on to potential clients. Leaving in the darkness before sunrise and feeling the insecurity of venturing off all by herself for the first time in her life, she designed a dummy to sit beside her in the passenger seat.

On her first day in Atlanta, she answered an advertisement in the *Atlanta Constitution*. The ad was for a housemate for a former school teacher who had just moved from North Carolina. The instant that Anna met Ann Ringland, she knew she had met a friend for life.

Several days later, Anna arrived at Sirius Talent, a top modeling agency in Atlanta. With her shoulder-length, permed hair, dressed in her best conservative school teacher attire, and carrying a large attractive handbag stuffed with everything but the kitchen sink, she entered the office of agent and owner Troy Davis. Troy, in his early forties, was quite handsome, slender, and very tall, at least six feet six, and very direct.

"So, you want to be a model?" Troy asked.

Trying not to let Troy's height and position of power intimidate her, Anna responded, "Yes, ever since I was a little girl, when I saw those ladies in the Sears and Roebuck catalog, I wanted to have a job like that." She didn't dare tell him how old she was before she found out that clothes could actually be bought in a store. And she certainly wasn't going to tell him that her early childhood wardrobe was fashioned from cow feed sacks by her mother on a Montgomery Ward sewing machine and she could even go with her parents to the feed store and help pick out the cow feed according to the design on the feed sack.

In a haughty manner, Troy replied, "Let me tell you what I expect of our models. I expect them to wear Anne Klein from head to toe. I expect them to have the most fashionable of hair styles. I do not like large handbags. I expect my models to carry a small fashionable purse. Any questions so far?"

Feeling very intimidated, while trying hard not to let it be obvious, Anna responded, "No, sir."

Troy handed her a business card and said, "I want you to test with Patrick Mackin. Here's his card. He's a fashion photographer here in Atlanta. Bring me the results.

At first, Anna didn't know what he meant by wanting her to test with Patrick Mackin, but then when he told her that Patrick was a fashion photographer, she realized that Troy wanted her to be photographed by Patrick, and the test was to see if her photographs would live up to the agency standards.

"Thank you, Mr. Davis," Anna responded trying very hard to maintain her composure.

By the way, Troy added in a condescending tone, "Our models don't call it a job when they model. They call it a booking."

Anna knew she could not afford to take Troy's comments personally. It would be real easy for her to turn tail and run. Instead, she interpreted every bit of the information that Troy gave her as clues to her future success as a model. Her next stop was at Atlanta's Lenox Mall. On her newly acquired credit card she purchased several Anne

Klein outfits, high fashion shoes, complementary earrings, black opaque stockings, and a small black purse. Several days later, she visited who was reputed to be the best hair stylist in Atlanta. She got her shoulder-length, permed hair, that had taken what seemed like forever to get the length she wanted it, cut and styled in a short, sleek look.

Several days later, Anna was at Patrick Mackin's house, having her hair and make-up done by a professional makeup artist for the first time in her life. What a treat! Having lost her mother at a very young age, she never knew what it was like to be pampered and spoiled over.

Patrick was a genius at matching a different location to each of Anna's outfits. One of her outfits was a red suit with a gold circular trim. For accessories she chose gold circular dangling earrings, black opaque panty hose, black spike heels and a small matching black purse. The location that Patrick chose for that outfit was outside what appeared to be an abandoned mall, except for few teenage boys hanging out. A red bench sat in the middle of a large area that was laid in large black and white tiles in a checkerboard pattern. He knew just how to utilize natural lighting and position Anna in a way that felt unnatural to say the least, but the results were fantastic.

The following week after Anna's photos were ready, she made an appointment with Troy Davis again. On the day of her appointment, the completely morphed Anna Weber entered Troy's office wearing a royal blue, fully lined, woolen Anne Klein skirt, turtleneck sweater, and complimentary gold jacket, black stockings and spike heels. She was carrying a small black purse, plus a manila envelope with the results of her photo shoot inside.

With the biggest most confident smile she said, "Good morning, Mr. Davis, I brought the results of my photo shoot."

A quizzical Troy responded, "Excuse me. I was expecting some else. Am I supposed to know you?"

"Yes, I was here two weeks ago," answered Anna.

Curiously Troy asked, "Refresh my memory?"

His response excited Anna, because she could tell he was much more pleased with her appearance than he had been when he met her several weeks earlier. She reminded him, "You wanted me to test with Patrick Mackin... Susan from The Millie Lewis Agency in Charleston made arrangements for me to see you."

A surprised Troy responded, "Oh, my, that was you? Let me see what you have."

Anna handed Troy the manila envelope with the photographs that Patrick Mackin had taken. Troy removed the photos and viewed them. Some were head-shots, some were three-quarter shots, and others were full-length. All were in Anne Klein and all are smashing! A most pleased Troy asked, "What's your name?"

"Anna Weber," Anna answered smugly.

Troy went to his door and requested that Anna follow him. He led her to the main office, where he caught the attention of his complete office staff, including his main booking agent, then proudly announced, "I want all of you to meet Anna Weber, our newest model."

Anna's next stop was at the department store at Lenox Mall. Wearing the same royal blue Anne Klein outfit that she had worn at Sirius Talent, she carried one large shopping bag and two garment bags. She handed the store clerk her receipts and the bags which contained the rest of the Anne Klein outfits. Sadly she informed the clerk, "I need to return these."

The clerk asked, "Is there anything wrong with them?"

Not wanting to tell the clerk that she couldn't afford the outfits and choking back her tears, because she had really grown attached to them, Anna simply said, "No, they're absolutely perfect. I wish I could keep them." The royal blue outfit and matching accessories she would keep to wear when she represented Sirius Talent.

The clerk responded, "If you'll give me your credit card, I'll credit your account."

"Thank you," Anna answered gratefully.

Was it a coincidence that Anna's first booking in Atlanta was for Sears? Remembering how she wished for it as a child, she didn't think so.

At the end of Anna's second year working out of Atlanta, she was on a runway booking, when she learned from one of the young models that modeling in Miami had made a comeback and was a great place to work. The model gave her the names and contact information of some of Miami's best agencies.

Anna also realized that if she worked in Miami, she would not have to commute year round like she did when working out of Atlanta. She would only have to be in Miami about half a year during what was known as 'the season' to the Miami modeling industry. The season was late fall, winter, and early spring when the weather was more favorable in Miami than anywhere else in the continental United States. She could be with her family during Thanksgiving and two weeks at Christmas, plus she and Richard could take turns flying back and forth to see each other on long weekends.

During the season, photographers, ad agents, and models came from all over the world and connected with the Miami talent agencies. The talent agencies matched the talent to the needs of the market, sometimes through direct bookings and other times through casting directors.

With revised childhood memories of her yearning to model in Miami and realizing that she would have more time to be with Richard if she only worked during the season, Anna mailed her headshots and composite cards to the agencies that the young model had recommended. Within days an agent named Dixie called her and said, "Come on down. Business is booming." Anna drove down to Miami, this time traveling alone without a dummy in the passenger seat, and when she arrived, Dixie was no longer working at the agency, but business was booming. Anna immediately registered with several of the best Miami agents and soon had more work than she had ever dreamed possible. Within a few months, while on a print booking for one of Jamaica's best vacation resorts, she found out she was chosen for that booking because she was considered a top model in her age category.

After a couple years of working in Miami, she cut her season in Miami short, so that she could work in New York for a few months each year. In New York she found ideal housing at Parkside Residence located at 13 Gramercy Park South. It was a hotel for women only, which operated under the auspices of the Salvation Army. There was a guard at the front entrance to thwart off male visitors. If a woman had a male visitor, he had to have clearance and she could only meet him in the parlor next to the front entrance in full view of the guard. When a couple of Anna's grandchildren visited her, her ten-year-old grandson, Benjamin, had to go through clearance too.

Her room on the fourteenth floor was about the size of her utility room at home and had a view of beautiful Gramercy Park below. Two meals a day were included in the cost of her room, breakfast and one other meal of her choice. She loved working in New York.

As a bright, beautiful, talented, and confident, five-feet-six-inch tall teenager, Sadie Leigh, wanted to be a model. She and her mother interviewed with Susan, owner of The Millie Lewis Agency. Claire had graduated from high school with Susan's husband Charlie. Claire told Susan that ever since Sadie was a little girl, people told her she should be a model.

Susan appreciated Sadie's clean wholesome look, because that's what they liked to promote at her agency. Susan recommended that Sadie compete in one of their conventions. Sadie would be seen by major talent agencies from around the world, as well as casting directors, talent managers, producers, and photographers.

Susan explained that Sadie would need intensive training at the studio. Training would be in runway, soap opera, situation comedy, swimsuit, photography, TV commercial, and talent. Training would be for three hours at a time, once a week for four months prior to the convention. Plus, she would be assigned a lot of homework.

Susan asked about Sadie's grades, because she didn't want training at the agency to interfere with her school work. Sadie promised her mother and Susan that she could keep her grades up and at the same time be totally committed to training for the convention. She also didn't want to disappoint her mother, because they would have to make the one-hundred-mile, round trip every week for Sadie to train at the agency.

Susan offered to take Claire and Sadie on a tour of the agency. The trio slowed down for a closer view of collages of photos on a main wall. Susan explained, "This is our Wall of Fame, where we display the work of some of our most successful talent. That's Ashley Scott. She was about your age, Sadie, when she trained for the convention. She became an international fashion model. She's also an actress. She recently landed the role of *Gigolo Jane* in Steven Spielberg's *Artificial Intelligence*.

"That's Anna Weber. She gave up a teaching career to start modeling and has done quite well."

"She looks familiar," responded Claire.

"You've probably seen her all over the place. You just didn't know who you were looking at," commented Susan. "She's been in local, national, and international commercials, done lots of print work for major magazines, travel brochures, and bill boards. Her permanent home is not far from here in Summerville, but she spends much of her time working mainly out of Miami and New York."

"Sadie, I can see you on Miss Susan's Wall of Fame," Claire remarked.

"That's a good goal to go for," Sadie agreed.

Four months later, Sadie did really well at the modeling convention. She received twenty-four callbacks. One of them was a New York agent, who invited her to audition for the soap opera *All My Children*. Claire drove Sadie to New York City to follow through with the invitation. Sadie was given a script to learn ahead of time. At sixteen, she was the youngest talent in the room of male and female actors whose ages were up to the mid-twenties.

Grimacing, Sadie told her mother, "I have knots in my stomach."

Claire advised her, "Take deep breaths. You've done all your preparatory work. There's nothing left to do but relax and enjoy it."

Sadie and a twenty-year-old man named Toby were called in to audition together. The casting director asked for their headshots, which the couple obligingly gave to him. He then gave them auditioning instructions and everything flowed smoothly.

A couple days later, Claire and Sadie, meet with the talent agent who invited them to New York, to get feedback from the soap opera audition. He reminded them that when Sadie competed at the convention, she blew everybody else away. He said, "I can see you in soap operas, movies, commercials, and more, but you will have to do several things. First, the only negative feedback I received was your southern accent. You will have to get rid of it."

Sadie agreed and he continued, "You will have to move to either New York or Los Angeles. My preference naturally is New York. Also, as talented as you are, you will still benefit from professional training."

Claire told him, "Right now our heads are spinning from all the positive interest in Sadie. Once things settle down, we'll make our decision."

The agent gave Claire his card and told her, "I hope to hear back from you." Then, addressing Sadie he said, "And to you young lady, work on getting rid of that southern accent."

Weeks later, Susan, Claire, and Sadie were in Florida interviewing with Miami agent Irena Gulbis. Proud that she had discovered the multi-talented teen sitting in front of her, Irena beamed, "Sadie, where do I start? Your performance at the convention was phenomenal. I've been in the business a long time and I know star quality when I see it!"

Sadie's response was, "Thank you. From you that's a real compliment."

When Irena asked how many callbacks Sadie got at the convention, Susan said it was twenty-four from all over, including New York, Los Angeles, Chicago, and Miami."

Irena was not at all surprised. Being very frank, she went straight to the point, telling Sadie, "You did great on runway. You got that walk down pat, but you don't have the height that the market requires." That comment was not a surprise to the trio.

Irena continued, "Sadie, your commercial audition was fabulous, but you need to get rid of your southern accent. Your photographs really caught my attention. I would love for you to test with one of Miami's best teen photographers, Steve Lattimore. How much longer will you be in Miami?"

Claire and Sadie agreed that they would like that very much and said they would be in town through Friday.

Irena immediately picked up the phone and left a message for Steve, "Hello Steve. Irena Gulbis here. I have this beautiful sixteen-year-old model in my office. She'll only be in town a couple days. Would you please, as a favor to me, make time in your busy schedule to have her test with you? Please give me a call asap."

Irena asked, "Now, Mrs. Porter how flexible are you? Would you be willing to move to Miami?"

Caught off guard, Claire responded, "I don't know."

Irena continued, "Our talent has to be where the action is. Our clients and casting directors would expect Sadie to show up at interviews and castings on short notice. You live, how far... six hundred miles from Miami?"

Claire answered, "Roughly, yes."

Irena explained, "Sadie has what it takes to make it big, but it can only happen if she lives where the work is. Think about it. Meanwhile, let's follow through with the photo shoot. I'll call you as soon as I hear from Steve."

Claire politely told Irena, "Thank you, Ms. Gulbis, you've given us a lot to think about."

Two days later, Claire and Susan observed Sadie as she had her photo session with the renowned photographer, Steve Lattimore. The results were fantastic.

In Lummus Park, formerly an old coconut plantation on Ocean Drive, next to the beach on South Beach, Miami, Ian, now forty, was visiting his mother and observing her in a photo shoot for a pharmaceutical advertisement. A small crew, including a makeup artist and wardrobe stylist, was helping photographer Reggie Blake take a series of photos of Anna, who was in her early 60s. She was walking a dog and interacting with the dog on the winding sidewalk that runs through the middle of the park.

When the photo shoot was over, Anna apologized to Ian for having to wait so long. He told her he enjoyed every minute of it. He had seen the results of her work for years, but had never seen her in action. They started walking and talking very slowly northward on the sidewalk, avoiding people walking, jogging, and rollerblading.

Ian remarked that the park was a perfect setting for a photo shoot and asked if that was where she made the Diesel Jeans advertisement that was in the *Rolling Stones* magazine years earlier. She responded, "No, that photo session was in Coral Gables." She added, "But I've had many photo shoots in this park." Pointing to a particular cluster of coconut trees, she recalled making a French commercial with a baby girl in fifty-five degree temperatures."

Showing concern, Ian commented, "They shouldn't have a baby out in the cold like that."

Anna explained, "We stayed bundled up until the actual filming time. She had a blanket wrapped around her and I held her real close to me to keep her warm. I thought I did a good job keeping her warm, until I received a copy of the commercial. Her little nose was red."

"I'm sure you enjoyed that job as much as you love babies," Ian responded.

Anna smiled telling him, "I always photograph best when I'm holding a baby."

Ian found that interesting. Anna spotted a bench and she and Ian sat down for a while.

"Whatever happened to Tara?" she asked.

Ian responded, "She married Doug Barrow."

"I saved her wedding announcement from the newspaper," offered Anna.

Curious, Ian asked her, "Why?"

"To put in a mini-photo album with pictures I took of Stephanie when she was two days old," she explained. "She might be gone, but she's still a part of my life."

Ian brought it to Anna's attention that in all the years since Stephanie was placed for adoption, they had never talked about her. She explained, "I've always kept my feelings to myself. You're like me like that." She paused and then told him, "I put a letter in her file at Social Services."

"I did too," Ian replied. "I put Mema and Papa's address in it, in case one day Stephanie looks at her file. Social Services will probably blacken it out, but if Stephanie looks at her file, she will at least know that she had a father who cared enough to try to leave contact information for her,"

"You really did care," Anna said with surprise.

Taken aback, Ian responded, "Of course I cared. She's my daughter."

Anna confessed, "All these years, I didn't realize how much you cared. I thought you were an irresponsible jock sowing his oats and didn't look back."

Disappointed, Ian responded, "I didn't know you had such a negative opinion of me."

"I'm so sorry," Anna apologized, "I guess I was so wrapped up in my own grief from losing Stephanie, I didn't fully realize what you were going through."

Ian revealed, "I've missed her every day of my life. I've watched her grow up in the faces of other girls her age. If I'm coaching a girl who I think has the slightest family resemblance, I find myself asking her when her birthday is."

Anna shared with him that she did that too when she worked in the school system. She paused, and then told him that sometimes she worried that Stephanie might have died like his sister, Wendy. She explained that while teaching she had several students die over the years for different reasons. When that happened she would pray for the family and then say an extra prayer for Stephanie wherever she was.

Ian told her, "Mom, I don't think I ever told you how relieved I was when I found out you stopped the abortion."

"I knew I couldn't live with myself if I didn't at least try to stop it," Anna responded. "I also knew that it would always be between us, if the abortion took place, because you tried to borrow money to pay for it."

Ian confessed, "I tried to stop the abortion too. Before you called and asked me to stop it, I was only thinking about what Tara wanted. She was extremely upset about what would happen if her family found out that she was pregnant. When I was unable to come up with the money for her to have the abortion, I thought she wouldn't have it. But somehow she came up with the money anyway and was able to keep her appointment. After you called me, I realized how much it would hurt you if she had the abortion. Plus, I didn't want it on my conscience the rest of my life. I tried to stop it, but I was told it was too late."

Anna told him, "We should have had this conversation years ago."

With relief and a hug, Ian told his mother, "I'm glad we're having it now."

At the south end of Lummus Park, Susan and Sadie were putting on roller blades. They were sitting on a bench facing the same winding sidewalk that Ian and Anna were facing further northward.

Sadie commented, "Miss Susan, you sure are a lot of fun."

Susan responded, "Experiencing rollerblading on South Beach is a must in Miami, second only to modeling."

Once their roller blades were secure, they stood up and Sadie announced, "C'mon, let's go." They rollerbladed northward for several blocks, right past and unnoticed by Anna and Ian who were still sitting on the bench talking. If Anna had been sitting at a different angle, she might have seen Susan and her beautiful teenage rollerblading companion.

Anna invited Ian to walk on the beach, saying, "You will love the beach here. It's much like the French Riviera."

CHAPTER 7

—— ❧ ——

Making Memories

A COUPLE WEEKS later, Sadie was spending the night with Susan at her country home. The two were sitting outside stargazing. They were both fascinated with stars. Susan commented that the stars might have a lot of answers to questions they don't even know yet. Sadie remarked that she had a question the stars can't answer.

When Susan questioned her about it, Sadie reminded her that she was adopted. She wondered where she came from, and what her background was.

Susan told her that she was also adopted, that when she was Sadie's age, she questioned her background a lot too. Years later, when she was grown, she searched until she found her biological family.

When Sadie questioned her about what she found, Susan told her it was bittersweet. "I found out that when I was in the ninth grade, my mother died in a state hospital from alcoholism. They didn't have alcohol treatment centers back then like they do now. Nobody knew who my father was, only that my mother didn't take responsibility for her children."

Sadie asked, "You had brothers and sisters?"

Susan replied, "I had twin brothers and one sister. I was the youngest. One twin died a few months before I made contact with my other brother and sister."

"Well, at least you found them," Sadie responded.

"Well, sort of," Susan explained, "The living twin wrote me a letter saying he had lost a brother, but was pleased he found a sister he didn't know he had. But he died of walking pneumonia before we had a chance to meet."

"How tragic," Sadie cried.

"The good part is I found my sister," Susan smiled.

Sadie questioned, "I wonder why my birth parents gave me away. Didn't they love me? Did they abandon me? Was I taken away from them because they were bad?" She paused and then added, "I sometimes wonder if I have any brothers and sisters and if I do, I wonder what they're like."

Susan responded, "I asked myself the same questions. I found out that when my siblings were born, my mother turned them over to my grandmother to raise. When she turned up pregnant with me, my grandmother convinced her to sign papers releasing me for adoption."

Sadie asked, "Do you regret searching for your birth family?"

Without hesitation Susan responded, "Not at all. I feel more blessed than ever to have been adopted."

Sadie confided, "I'm afraid of what I might find out if I find mine."

Susan wisely told her, "That's normal. But remember, what you find might be good too. If you ever decide to search, I'll be glad to help you."

Months later, Susan and her husband invited well over 100 guests to a Christmas party at their home, which included southern pork barbeque, lots of home baked goodies, and a live, three-piece band playing on their large patio. Anna always enjoyed slow dancing and shagging with Richard to 50's music. On this occasion, after a few good dances, the band changed to playing Billy Ray Cyrus' *Achy Breaky Heart*. Suddenly, about a half dozen adolescents came running from the large food tent, ran to the dance floor, and started line dancing. Anna loved the music, but wasn't about to line dance to it, not with her two left feet. She was quite contented to just stand on the sidelines watching the young teens dancing, not realizing that one of them was Stephanie to her.

Some of Anna's most special times were centered around her grandchildren's visits during their summer vacation. On one such occasion, she was driving them to the community swimming pool on the opposite end of her subdivision. Her nine-year-old granddaughter, McKenna, was seated in the front passenger seat. Her six-year-old grandson Ryan, the youngest of Ian's four children, was seated in the back seat right behind McKenna. Anna had the right of way as they approached an intersection. She could see that there was no way the driver of a speeding car approaching them on the passenger side of her car would be able to stop for their stop sign. She slammed on her brakes to avoid being hit. She followed the car for a short distance.

Confused because of the change of direction, McKenna remarked, "Oma, this is not the way to the swimming pool."

"I know," Anna responded, "I have some business to tend to first."

When the car that had been speeding pulled into a driveway and stopped, she followed it. A man in a business suit got out and started walking hurriedly toward the back door to a house. Anna got out of her car and yelled, "You just wait one darn minute!"

Turning around and facing Anna, the man started walking backward slowly toward the house as he excused himself by saying, "I know. I should have stopped."

That not being good enough, Anna tried to shame him by the seriousness of the situation, "My grandchildren were on the passenger side of my car! I don't appreciate you putting them in that kind of danger."

A more meek response from the man who was now stopped dead in his tracks was, "I am so very sorry."

Anna responded firmly, "You ought to be!"

At the community pool a few minutes later, Anna was seated on the side of the pool. McKenna was swimming in the deep water. Ryan was in the shallow end of the pool when he asked Anna, "Oma, why is McKenna swimming in the deep water and I can't?"

Anna responded, "I've seen her swim in the deep end before, but I've never seen you swim in deep water." She paused and then asked, "Have you ever swum in deep water?"

"No, but I know I can," Ryan said with confidence.

Anna struck up a bargain, "I tell you what. If you can swim or tread water in the shallow end here for five minutes without touching bottom, I'll let you swim in the deep end."

"That's easy," assured Ryan.

When the clock on the side of the pool building indicated that five minutes was up, Ryan proudly asked, "Oma, can I swim in the deep end now? Five minutes is up." Anna gave him the thumbs up. "Absolutely. You did good."

When Anna's grandson John was fifteen, Ian took him fishing for crappie and bream off of a Lake Keowee dock. "John, I learned all I know about fishing from my Granddaddy Bierer," Ian reminisced.

"I wish I had known him," responded John, "He died a month before I was born."

"He was his own person, soft spoken, never said much, but when he did, he got people's attention and respect. He was an assistant state veterinarian and worked in an experimental laboratory, trying to find cures for diseases in chickens, turkeys, and other fowl," explained Ian.

"He must have been very smart," John answered with pride.

Ian proceeded to tell him the story of his grandfather's retirement dinner. "When he was sixty-five, he was forced to retire because it was the mandated retirement age for state employees. During his career, he had received all kinds of awards, was guest speaker at the World Poultry Congress in Australia, all kinds of good things. At his retirement dinner everybody he worked with had a chance to get up and say great things about him. When they were all finished, he stood up and with a straight face, he calmly said, "If I'm so darn good, why are you getting rid of me?" and sat down. There was a moment of stunned silence, followed by a roar of laughter."

"That's just too cool!" laughed John.

Ian added, "They hired him back as a consultant." Ian paused, and hesitantly said, "John there's something I've been wanting to talk to you about."

John asked, "What's that?"

Ian continued, "Before I married your mom, I had a relationship with a very special young woman. As a result of that relationship, you have a half-sister out there somewhere."

Startled, John said, "Whoa! I do? I wasn't expecting that!"

Ian continued, "Yeah, it's true. Her name is Stephanie. She was born two years before you. She was placed for adoption." With a faraway look, he added, "Her mother was a very special lady."

John asked, "Why didn't you marry her?"

"We broke up," Ian explained, "and by the time I found out she was pregnant, I was engaged to your mom. The rest is history."

"Where is she? Is she still in the area?" John asked curiously.

"No, she moved out of the area a long time ago," Ian responded. "The last I heard, her husband's job moved them to a small town outside of Asheville."

"No," John corrected his father, "I wasn't asking about the lady you got pregnant, I was asking where is my half sister? Is she still in the area? What if I end up dating her, not knowing she's my sister?"

Ian explained that he didn't know where Stephanie was, that her mother requested she be adopted out of the area. Because of the mobile society we live in, she could be living down the street or in California or anywhere in between. If she was adopted by a military family, she could be anywhere in the world.

"Hey, this means I'm not your first born," John remarked sounding a bit disappointed for losing that status.

Ian answered reassuringly, "Well, yeah, but I love you still the same."

CHAPTER 8

A Blessed Life

SADIE'S TEEN YEARS were ideal. Her adoptive family always gave her every opportunity to lead the fullest, most well rounded life possible. She had a strong Christian upbringing and the love and guidance of a large extended family. She also enjoyed family activities such as water skiing at Lake Marion and snow skiing at the Snowshoe Lodge in Silver Creek, West Virginia. She enjoyed caring for and riding her paint horse named Charlie. She even enjoyed hunting for white tail deer with her father.

She attended a private high school with the reputation of having the highest academic standards in the county. Her entire curriculum was college prep. She had a part-time job tutoring in her school's homework center.

She was admired and respected by her teachers, her peers, and her community. In sports she was captain of her volleyball team, on the basketball and softball teams. She was also a cheerleader, homecoming queen and May Court Queen.

One day in the spring of her senior year in high school, as president of her school's Student Council, Sadie represented her school at a state meeting held near the State

Capitol in Columbia. After the meeting, she returned to her part-time job at school.

After tutoring, Sadie was driving her 1994 red Saturn toward her home. The Norfolk Southern Railroad crossing near her home was up and over a hill. Trees and brush blocked the view to the right. There was no arm to come down and stop traffic, and the flashing signal lights were not working. There was a pickup truck in front of her and a car behind her. As she started crossing the tracks, the truck in front of her suddenly braked for a stop sign. She slammed on her brakes. A train whistle blared. As Sadie looked to the right to see the train that was going to hit her, she felt the presence of a guardian angel. In vain, she accelerated as hard as she could. The sound of metal on metal was overpowered by the roar of the freight train.

It took a while, but the long train finally came to a stop. The engineer ran back to the crossing. He was horrified because he had recognized the car that he had just hit as that of the pretty young girl who had been waving at him for the past fifteen years. A small crowd gathered.

A middle-aged woman who was in the car behind Sadie tearfully said, "That could have been me! Those warning lights were not flashing. I'm certain of that. There was no warning! All of a sudden the train whistled and it hit her. It happened so fast!"

They couldn't find the car. Law enforcement had not arrived yet, but the fire chief happened on the scene. The engineer cried out, "She must have gotten dragged under the train." He and those who had gathered started looking under the train.

A short while later, Claire drove up to the scene with Sadie, who was in shock and uncontrollably jerking, in her passenger seat. The fire chief approached Claire's car and when he saw Sadie he exclaimed, "Oh my God! This has got to be some kind of miracle. We thought you were dead."

Claire explained, "Our neighbor, Joshua Adams, found her back down on the side of the road in hysterics and brought her to me. Can I take her to Bryan's office to get her to calm down?"

Still shaking his head in disbelief, the fire chief told Sadie, "You don't know how lucky you are to be alive, young lady." And to Claire he said, "Of course you can take her to Bryan's office. We know where to find you."

After she calmed down, Sadie told her mother that the only thing she remembered after she saw the train was going to hit her was she felt the presence of a guardian angel. Fortunately, Sadie escaped injury, but the rear of her car was heavily damaged.

Even though the fire chief had given Clare permission to take Sadie to Bryan's office to get her to calm down, Sadie was charged with leaving the scene of the accident. Rather than dispute the charge in court, Sadie's family was so relieved that she was not seriously hurt or killed, they paid the fine and put the whole incident behind them. After the accident, the family was glad to see Norfolk Southern cut down all the trees and brush that blocked the view of approaching trains at that railroad crossing, and the crossing signal was repaired.

Before the accident, living so near the railroad tracks, Sadie had become so accustomed to the train whistle that she never paid much attention to it, but for a long time after the accident, hearing the train whistle would send her into a panic.

After Sadie graduated from high school, she attended the university two hundred miles away from home, where she lived on campus and majored in psychology. In her senior year, she found an apartment off campus across the Saluda River near Rivermont Park. She shared her apartment with Carolina, her white Maltese puppy. It was an ideal place for Sadie to keep fit by walking and jogging along the trails in the park bordering the river.

At the end of her senior year, one of her classes in social work was on the topic of adoption. She learned that when someone releases their child for adoption, Social Services would permit them to put a letter containing non-identifiable information in their child's file. This peaked Sadie's curiosity. She called her mother and to her surprise, her mother told her that the day she and her father adopted her, the caseworker at Social Services gave them letters that were written to her by her birth parents. They were advised to wait until she was at least twenty-one before giving the letters to her. The letters were in a safety deposit box.

Right after that, Sadie graduated and moved to an apartment in Summerville. As part of her housewarming, her mother brought her a manila envelope. Inside the envelope was the file that Social Services had given her and Mike the day they adopted Sadie. Sadie pored over the information, but there wasn't anything in the file that would help satisfy her curiosity. Her mother told her there was a second file, sealed by the court, that it would be available to her now that she had reached the age of twenty-one.

CHAPTER 9

Too Close
For Comfort

ON FRIDAY, SEPTEMBER 7, 2001, Anna was in New York City on a photo shoot for a print booking for a denture cream advertisement. She was being filmed in a studio, with a man in his early sixties, plus a couple in their early forties. They were in a family dinner scene, laughing and pretending to eat corn on the cob.

That evening, Anna was staying in a seventh floor apartment at 333 Rector Place in Battery Park City, a residential area, facing the Hudson River, a block from the World Trade Center. Her friends, Vickie and Bob Cooper, let her use their apartment while they were out of town.

She viewed the skyline over the Hudson from a window, while making a phone call to Richard.

"Honey, I need to stay over until Monday. There's a writing class at the Screen Actors Guild that I want to attend. I don't think I'll have any problem changing my ticket to a later flight. When is your business trip to Detroit? The eleventh? Good, at least we'll see each other for a few hours before you leave. Take care and remember I love you."

Monday morning was chilly and rainy. Anna, was wearing a trench coat with a hood. She and her friend, Pat Jones, were walking up Broadway toward Time Square. Pat was a fellow senior citizen model who also attended classes at the Screen Actors Guild. Anna was not as lonesome working in New York when Pat was around.

Pat, whose permanent home was in Florida, commented on them being fortunate to have two very understanding husbands. Anna agreed, reflecting how Richard, who never had any dreams or goals of his own, was super understanding. His life just fell into place beautifully. She shared with Pat how Richard once told her, "I don't understand why you're doing what you're doing," referring to her traveling to work as a model and actress, "but I understand that you have to do it." She added, "That had more meaning to me than anything he has ever told me."

Anna told Pat how much she enjoyed her writing class at the Guild. She added, "Mark Weston teaches my writing class. He was the original Brylcreem man on TV back in the 1950s. Remember those commercials where a good looking guy with great hair would be on the screen and a jingle would sing 'a little dab'l do you' and 'they love to get their fingers in your hair' while a pretty girl would be stroking his hair? Well, he writes plays and documentaries now. He's a fantastic teacher."

The two ladies approached a large crowd with concerned looks on their faces. As they pushed through the crowd, they heard a voice saying, "Somebody ought to do something." Some people just stood staring down toward the same direction, while others walked away. Anna heard someone say an ambulance had been called.

She looked over the shoulders of some spectators and saw a middle-aged white man dressed in a business suit lying unconscious face down in a gutter full of water. A briefcase was beside him. It flashed through Anna's mind that the crowd was letting the man drown in the gutter while waiting for the ambulance. Time was of the essence, so she dashed over to the man and struggled to pull him out of the gutter. He was heavy. She screamed at the crowd, "Somebody help me!" A man came from the crowd and together they started pulling the man out of the water.

"Not on his face," Anna hollered. They turned the man over on his back and continued removing him from the gutter. The man's face was blue. Anna took off her trench coat and covered him and sat down beside him. The man who helped her disappeared into the crowd. By the time an ambulance arrived, about five minutes later, the man's coloring had returned to normal, but he was still unconscious. One of the medics removed Anna's trench coat from the man and gave it to her, telling her that they would take over from there. She told him that the man had been blue.

After the medics loaded the man in the ambulance, Anna and Pat resumed their walk up Broadway. Pat said, "I never saw anybody save a life before."

Anna felt bad because she didn't have the medical knowledge to help the man. She didn't even know how to take his pulse.

The next morning will be implanted in Anna's memory forever. It was Tuesday, September 11, 2001, a clear and sunny day with a bright blue sky and she was at home, having arrived on the last flight to the Charleston airport around midnight the night before. Richard carried a garment bag and pulled his carry-on suitcase to their front door. Anna remarked, "We're like two ships passing in the night. I just flew back from Manhattan and you're flying to Detroit."

Richard promised her he would call her as soon as he arrived in Detroit. She told him to travel safe and to remember she loved him as he pulled out of their driveway, heading to the airport.

Fifteen minutes later, Richard burst in their front door, dropping his carry-on suitcase and garment bag on the floor. "You don't have the TV on?" he asked excitedly.

When Anna asked what was wrong, as he was turning on the TV, he told her, "All flights are canceled. Two airplanes crashed into the Twin Towers. Reports are calling it a terrorist attack!" News accounts of the planes crashing into the Twin Towers and the Pentagon were on the TV.

When Richard told Anna how grateful he was that she came home when she did, she remembered how she had just gone shopping in one of the Twin Towers the day before. Suddenly, she could see the faces of two different clerks who had waited on her when she made two separate purchases at the Banana Republic in one of the towers. One was an attractive young black woman and the other was a tall slender older white man with white hair. She wondered if they survived. While watching the news, she got sick to her stomach.

After Anna collected her thoughts, she became worried about her friends who had let her use their New York apartment near the World Trade Center. They were supposed to return to their apartment within hours after she left.

She found out later, they were away from their apartment when the attacks happened and were not permitted to return home because their apartment building had been roped off as part of a crime scene. It wasn't until late December after 9/11 that they were permitted to return to their apartment, which was covered with four inches of ash from the collapse of the towers.

Anna decided to rewrite her will to include Stephanie as one of her beneficiaries. While doing so she also wrote an updated letter to be placed in Stephanie's file. In it she told Stephanie about what was currently going on in Ian's life and she wrote a brief description of each one of Ian's other four children without revealing any names or geographical locations, but she did slip in a few more clues here and there. She was hoping that if Stephanie ever read the letter, that the knowledge that she had four half siblings would entice her to search for them and in doing so, would find her.

She also told Stephanie, "I changed my career from teaching to modeling, something I always wanted to do when I grew up. The one thing that hasn't changed is my hope that one day you will be a part of my life. I love you wherever you are," and she signed it, "Your Grandmother."

In her letter to the Department of Social Services she wrote:

> To Whom It May Concern;
> Enclosed is another letter to put in my grand-daughter's file. She was born Stephanie Lynn Harper on June 21, 1983. Also, would you please let me know how I should go about leaving something for Stephanie in my will?
> Thank you,
> Anna Weber

CHAPTER 10

Ian Tells McKenna

THREE YEARS LATER, Ian and his fourteen-year-old daughter, McKenna. were walking trails at Rivermont Park near their home. They stopped at a bench facing the river. McKenna sat down while Ian stayed standing admiring the rapids on the Saluda River below.

Taking advantage of the moment McKenna asked, "Dad, can we go to Disney World during Easter break?"

Ian explained that trips like that would take time to plan and she should have asked a long time ago. Her response was, "What's to plan? Just bring a tooth brush and clean underwear."

She continued to plead her case. With her many years experience of wrapping her father around her little finger, she said, "Aw, come on, how can you say 'no' to your only little princess?"

With that Ian sat down beside her and asked her, "What if I told you that you're not my only little princess?"

McKenna responded, "Oh, but I am."

Ian took a deep breath and told her, "No, I have another little princess out there somewhere."

"What are you talking about?" McKenna demanded.

Ian responded, "Years ago, before I married your mother, I dated a girl I cared for a lot, but we broke up and by the time I found out she was pregnant, I was engaged to your mom."

McKenna asked, "Why didn't you tell me sooner? Isn't that something I should have known?"

"I wanted to wait until you were old enough to understand," he responded.

"What's her name?" asked McKenna.

Looking rather melancholy, he told her, "Stephanie, Stephanie Lynn."

Curious, McKenna commented, "Gee, I wonder what she's like."

Ian told her he wondered what Stephanie was like all the time. He sometimes wondered if he made a mistake signing the release to give her up. But then, if he had not, McKenna's mom would not have married him and he wouldn't have her for his daughter.

McKenna consoled him, "I hope you find her one day or she finds you. I always wanted a big sister."

CHAPTER 11

The Search

FOUR YEARS LATER, In May of 2010, at the modern two-story country home of Claire and Bryan Porter, twenty-seven year-old Sadie had just arrived to get ready for her wedding. Carrying her wedding gown, she was accompanied by her twenty-nine-year-old step-sister Hope and her good friend Emma. Hope was armed with a makeup case, and Emma was carrying a camera. All three were dressed in tank tops, capris, and sandals.

Sadie's mother wasn't home, so she asked her stepfather, Bryan, if they could use their master bedroom for her to get ready for her wedding. Bryan told her she could use their bedroom, only if he could wear a powder blue leisure suit to her wedding. He had been on her case about wearing a powder blue leisure suit to her wedding for the past few months, because he never liked wearing a tuxedo. Sadie reminded him that her wedding was a formal affair. But Bryan insisted that she allow him to wear a powder blue leisure suit. To humor him Sadie smiled and told him, "Okay Bryan, you can wear a powder blue leisure suit. Now can we use your bedroom to get ready?"

With that, he smiled back and nodded at her saying, "Just make yourself at home."

On the way up the stairs, Emma, looked concerned and asked, "Was he really serious?"

Sadie laughingly remarked, "No way, he's just kidding."

Emma started snapping pictures the time they entered the master bedroom, starting with Sadie hanging her wedding gown on the back of the door. Sadie sat on a stool at the master dressing table. Hope pinned Sadie's hair on top of her head in preparation for styling it after she finished applying her makeup. She started to apply Sadie's makeup and stopped, declaring, "This lighting here is absolutely the worst! A woman's makeup has to be perfect on her wedding day. We have to go somewhere else."

Sadie moved the stool to a spot near a window where there was more natural lighting. Hope said, "This is better, but it's still not good enough either. Where's the best lighting in the house?"

Emma announced, "The lighting in the bathroom is awesome." The bathroom was very spacious, with an oversized tub in a corner with large windows on two sides. Emma added, "And the natural lighting by the bathtub is the best of all." Sadie looked at Hope, and Hope looked at Sadie, and in unison they said, "Let's go for it!" Sadie climbed into the tub and Hope followed her and proceeded to apply Sadie's makeup as Emma was capturing one Kodak Moment after another.

Reminisce is the name of an elegant facility, including a reception hall and pond, in the country for weddings, receptions, and family reunions. Twenty minutes before Sadie's wedding was scheduled to take place,

Emma, dressed in her hot pink bridesmaid dress, was still taking pictures. Claire, dressed as mother-of-the-bride in a royal blue, tea-length, chiffon dress, was on her cell phone. "Hope, are you finished with Sadie's hair yet? Good, bring her over here to me. Her surprise is ready."

Claire stepped out of view from the door that Sadie would be entering and Bryan took her place. When Sadie entered the room, the first thing she saw was Bryan dressed in a powder blue leisure suit, white shirt, no tie, white shoes, and a white hat with a wide brim. Emma captured Sadie's surprised reaction on camera.

Sadie's wedding was like out of a fairy tale. She was radiant with her long locks swept up gracefully on top of her head, with a few loose strands framing her face.

Her groom, tall, dark, and handsome Barrett Chambers, dressed in a gray tuxedo, was her Prince Charming since childhood. When she was in the second grade she declared that she was going to marry him when she grew up.

The ceremony, witnessed by over three-hundred guests, took place on the banks of the pond. The nine bridesmaids, including Hope, Emma, and Adrienne wore hot pink dresses, and the eleven groomsmen all wore gray tuxedos. They had a live band and dancing on the lawn under strings of paper lanterns. Included in the abundance of hot and cold hor d'oeuvres, was Sadie's favorite, boiled peanuts, a true southern delicacy.

Sadie and Emma worked together at an attorney's office in a larger town about thirty minutes away. They solved a lot of the world problems, as well as their own, during their thirty minute commute through country roads of pines and scrub oaks. There was always the possibility of hitting wild animals, including white tail deer, when driving on the back roads. On one stretch of the road they took every day was a wide path opened by a tornado several years earlier. In nearby tree tops that were not directly affected by the tornado, pink fiberglass insulation ripped from homes several miles away was still clinging to branches.

When Emma was driving on one of these early morning commutes, she asked Sadie why she looked so rough.

Sadie told her she was up half the night. To that Emma gave her an all knowing smile and said, "I know you're a newlywed, but you and Barrett have to come up for air some time."

Sadie chuckled, "It's not that. I was searching for my birth parents on the web." She confided that she had searched on and off since high school, but never found anything. Ever since she and Barrett got married, her interest in finding her roots had grown stronger.

Emma asked her what she could do differently. Sadie told her that when she was at the university, she took a course in social work. In one of the classes where the topic was adoption, she learned that, after an adoption had taken place, the files of adoptions were sealed. The file would remain sealed unless the child who was adopted requested that it be opened for them, after they reached the age of twenty-one. "I don't know why I haven't asked for my file. Momma also told me about it after I turned twenty-one, but I couldn't bring myself to do anything about it." Sadie paused and then added, "To tell you the truth, I'm afraid of what I might find."

After chatting about it for some time, Emma agreed to call Social Services for Sadie. She did, but was told that Sadie herself would have to submit a written request for her file and include a check for a fee. With Emma's encouragement, Sadie mustered up the courage to request her file.

With the realization that she had actually asked for her file and she might find her biological family, Sadie became extremely upset. She didn't want to hurt her adoptive parents. She had worked herself into a complete frenzy by the time she arrived at her Aunt Janet's house. Aunt Janet, who was married to Sadie's mother's youngest brother, had been a long time mentor to Sadie.

Sadie cried, "I started my search for my biological parents today. I called Social Services and they're going to send me my file."

"So what's the problem?" her aunt asked.

"I don't want to hurt Momma. I don't want her to think I'm trying to replace her and Daddy," Sadie explained.

Aunt Janet firmly told her, "You couldn't replace them even if you tried. They are your mother and father."

"I know I'm not trying to replace them, but they might not know that," Sadie argued.

"I promise you," Janet reassured her, "you will not hurt your Momma. She has always told you she would stand behind you if you ever wanted to search for them, now hasn't she?"

"Yes, ma'am," Sadie agreed.

"Why do you think she gave you that packet of information after you turned twenty-one? That was her granting her permission for you to search if you ever decided to. So quit fretting over it and go talk to your Momma... right now." Aunt Janet insisted.

"But..." Sadie protested.

"Sadie," Aunt Janet said firmly, "you go talk to her, tell her what you just told me. Your momma won't be hurt by it. Trust me."

Sadie's next stop was at her mother's house, where she found Claire sitting on her front porch swing. Sadie sat down to join her and immediately burst into tears.

"Before I say anything else, I want you to know I love you and Daddy, and nobody could ever take your place," she sobbed.

"I know that," Claire acknowledged.

"I contacted Social Services today and they're going to send me a copy of my file. I'm going to seriously search for my biological family," she confessed.

"Sadie, I'm fine with that," Claire told her with confidence. "I've always told you I'd support you one-hundred percent, if you ever wanted to search for them. We have a bond nobody can break. But keep in mind, you don't know what you'll find. You don't know if your birth parents have told their families that you even exist."

Seven weeks later, on a Wednesday in mid-August, Sadie received a notice from the post office saying she needed to sign for some registered mail from the Department of Social Services. She notified her boss that she would be running late on Thursday and let Emma know that she wouldn't be riding with her to work.

The next morning, she stopped by the post office on the way to work. As much as she tried to maintain her composure, when the postal clerk handed her a large manila envelope, he commented on how nervous she was. After exiting the post office, she sat in her car outside, opened the envelope, and glanced through the contents to make sure it was indeed her adoption file.

When she arrived at the law firm where she worked, she was carrying the manila envelope with the secrets of her adoption file in it. She went straight to her office, picked up her phone and buzzed Emma, whose office was upstairs.

A few minutes later, Emma entered Sadie's office, accompanied by co-workers Amy, Debbi, and Diana, and they all gathered around Sadie's desk. Sadie excitedly told them, "You sure didn't waste any time."

"Bless our wise bosses," Amy responded. "When you called, they said they knew we wouldn't be able to focus on getting any work done until we know what's in your file and start helping you with your search."

Diana offered, "Just let us know what you want us to do."

Sadie directed, "I'll read and you see if you notice any clues that might help locate my biological parents."

She picked up the first item in the stack of documents.

It was her birth certificate. She looked over it and handed it to Debbi. Debbi looked at it and remarked, "Hmm, you were born Stephanie? That's one of my favorite names."

Emma commented, "She looks like Sadie to me."

Sadie said, "This letter is from my birth mother. It says,

'To my Baby Girl, Your father and I love you very much. I'm only eighteen, with no job and your father's job doesn't pay much. I prayed that God would place you with loving and caring parents. I can't see you, or watch over you, but I know He can. I also pray every night that maybe one day when you are old enough, God will bring us together and I can see you again. God brought you into this world for a reason. You were not a mistake. Maybe your parents prayed very hard for you and God worked through me to answer their prayers. I love you and am always thinking of you. Your Mother.'"

With tears in her eyes Diana observed, "That was very mature for an eighteen-year-old."

"But unfortunately it didn't have the first clue," noted Debbi.

Sadie handed the letter to one of her friends.

Attorney Roger Bledsoe stuck his head in the door.

"How are you ladies doing?"

Sadie responded, "We're all feeling a little bit Nancy Drewish at the moment."

Amy told him, "The only thing we found out so far is Sadie's birth name was Stephanie."

"She looks like Sadie to me. Let me know if I can be of any help," he responded before leaving the ladies alone in their search for clues.

Sadie continued, "This letter is from my father. "Dear Stephanie, I honestly hope that the decision that your mother and I made was the right one. Your mother is one of the sweetest, most beautiful women God ever graced the Earth with. We had a beautiful summer romance and broke up. By the time I found out Tara was pregnant, I was engaged to someone else...'"

Emma interrupted, "Ah-ha, clue number one. Your mother's name was Tara."

Sadie continued, "The two hardest things I've ever had to do in my life were to give you up and to tell the woman I planned to marry that someone else was pregnant with my child. I've already found myself looking at babies and wondering if they might be you. Please try to find your mother and try to find me. My most likely permanent address would be through my grandparents. Send to my name at...' Sadie stopped reading and told her friends that the rest had been whitened out.

Sadie examined the letter. "Part of the address is still here. There's a 'Ave' and 'SC.' There must be thousands of avenues in South Carolina." Sadie handed the letter to one of the ladies.

She picked up another document. "This Social Services report says the mother had sex once and used no form of birth control."

"Birth control was not as readily available back then like it is now," offered Diana.

"Mama said people back then didn't talk about anything that had to do with sex. It was all hush-hush," added Emma.

"And women had to ask the pharmacist for a contraception. It was embarrassing, because the pharmacists were usually men and they would give the woman an all knowing smile, because they knew she was planning to do 'it'," offered Amy.

"And if any one saw her making the purchase... heaven forbid... it would be the talk of the town," contributed Debbi.

Breathing a sigh of relief Diana chirped, "Today we have a more realistic attitude toward sex. Thank goodness."

"Reality is... it only takes one time to get pregnant," shared Emma.

Knowing her parent's situation, Sadie told them, "That's only if you're fertile. My parents tried for years to get pregnant. They tried everything in the book, including hormone treatments. You name it, they tried it."

Sadie continued to read the Social Service report. "Let's see... this says 'The mother's father was upset when he found out his daughter was pregnant. He threatened to make her leave home, unless she went away to have the baby and release it for adoption. The baby's father wanted her to keep his baby. He also spoke of trying to obtain custody of the baby. The baby's mother also has been dating a young man who is accepting of the situation and supports her in her decision to place her baby for adoption."

She handed the report to one of the ladies.

Amy shook her head and said, "This is sounding more and more like a soap opera."

Sadie picked up another document. With a quizzical look she said, "Here's another letter. 'Dear Stephanie, I got to hold you when you were two days old to say both hello and good-bye to you. I even got to take your picture. Your pictures I will always cherish.'" Sadie paused.

"Wait... I wonder who this is from?" She flipped to the next page and told them, "This is signed from my grandmother," and then she returned to the first page and continued reading.

"Somehow, in this letter I'm supposed to replace the special moments in our lives that we should have been able to share, but can't. I am your grandmother, your father's mother. There are several people I'd like to introduce you to. First is your great-grandfather, my father..." Sadie stopped reading and explained, "Social Services whitened out a lot here," she then continued, "He wrote books about Indians and Artifacts in the Southeast."

"That's the kind of information we need," interrupted Emma.

Sadie continued, "He is a poultry pathologist and was chosen Veterinarian-of-the-Year in the 1960's and was a guest speaker at the World Poultry Congress held in... that's been whitened out, too."

Amy piped in, "Probably not too many poultry pathologists who wrote books about Indian artifacts. With a little cross referencing we should easily discover who he is."

"There's more," Sadie added, "'His wife died of leukemia at age 31, leaving him with seven children between the ages of thirteen years and five months. I am the middle of his seven children.' This has got one clue after another. This looks like some real good stuff!"

With a more somber tone Emma interjected, "Can you imagine what it was like for his wife to die at age thirty-one and leave seven little kids behind?"

Diana said, "That's heavy."

Sadie read further, "I will now tell you something special about each of my siblings and myself. My oldest brother built the world's largest heart-shaped swimming pool..."

Debbi interrupted, "I can research heart-shaped swimming pools for you."

"That would be wonderful," Sadie responded gratefully. She then turned the next page. "Huh! Wait a minute. Two pages are missing, pages two and three. All this page says is, 'Stephanie, I'm saving your mother's letters for you. I can't ever give up hope. Maybe one day I can at least see you as a bride and perhaps spoil my first great-grand- child as I wanted to spoil you. God knows how much I love you and want you as a part of my life. Affectionately, Your Grandmother.'" She paused and then said, "I wonder what letters from my mother she was talking about."

"Aw," Amy said sadly, "She just missed your wedding."

With a smile, Sadie responded, "If she's still alive and we find her, it won't be too late for her to spoil my babies."

Emma, with a bigger smile asked, "Your babies? Is there something you haven't told us?"

"Like what?" Sadie asked and then she realized what Emma was implying, "Oh, no I'm not pregnant, but I plan to be."

Emma questioned, "I wonder what happened to the two missing pages."

"That's okay," Sadie told her confidently, "I think we have all the information we need to go on for now."

On that same hot mid-August morning, a couple hundred miles away, Ian was driving his son Ryan to school. Ryan was a sophomore in high school and was on the school's swim team. He'd come a long way with his swimming since the summer Anna had let him swim in the deep end of her community's swimming pool.

Ian shared with him that this was the first time in twenty years he had to drive only one child to school. He added that there were some years that he and Ryan's mom had to drive all four of their children to four different schools. Ryan said it made him feel special to be the youngest child in his parents' nest. "But," he added, "I really appreciate having three siblings. By watching them, it helped me learn what to do and not to do. Like John being the oldest, he got fussed at a lot."

"He's the one your mom and I learned how to be parents by," offered Ian.

"Miles never caused any trouble," Ryan added, "He's always focused. He's more the intellectual type. And McKenna, she's got it made. She's good looking, intelligent, and being your only daughter, she knows how to wrap you around her little finger."

Hesitantly, Ian told him, "What if I told you McKenna is not your only sister?"

Jokingly, Ryan responded, "I'd say either you or Mom would have some explaining to do."

Taking a deep breath, Ian explained, "It's me that has the explaining to do. You have a half-sister named Stephanie. I didn't know her mother was pregnant until after I was engaged to your mom. I had to give up my rights to her before I could marry your mom."

"That's sad. I'm sorry to hear that, but I'm glad you married Mom," replied Ryan.

"Me too," agreed Ian, "or I wouldn't have you.

"How old is she?" Ryan asked curiously.

His dad responded, "Twenty-seven. Over the years, I've watched her grow up in the faces of young girls and now young women." With a faraway look he said, "She's a part of me that's always missing."

Sadie and Barrett's starter home was an adorable English cottage style, meticulously landscaped with evergreen shrubs and flowers of varying colors. Due to Sadie's green thumb, their flowers were still magnificent in spite of the August heat.

Determined to locate her biological family, she situated herself on a comfortable living room chair with her iPad, writing pad, pen, glass of wine, snacks, and a blanket. Her supportive, but partially skeptical husband, watched TV while she researched.

Sadie called, "Hey Barrett, I found my great-grandfather."

Barrett turned off the TV and joined her by sitting on the arm of her chair. Looking over her shoulder, he curiously asked, "Who is he? How did you find him?"

Proudly, Sadie responded, "Actually, it was easy. At work we made a computer printout of authors of American Indian books. We were prepared to research the whole list if necessary. His name was near the top of the list when I started searching earlier this evening. Dr. Bert Bierer was the only veterinarian on the list. He's deceased. He wrote a number of books. One was titled, *Indians and Artifacts in the Southeast.* My grandmother wrote that in her letter to me, but she didn't italicize it or underline it as the name of a book. If she had, the Department of Social Services would have blackened it out, because it could have easily identified him. It's got to be him."

As he rubbed her shoulders Barrett's response was, "I am so proud of you. That's wonderful. Now will you come to bed? I'm ready to hit the sack."

Sadie was torn. She wanted to join him in bed, but felt like the answers to her heritage were just minutes away. "I'll be there in a little while."

Barrett reminded her, "You have to go to work in the morning."

"Yeah, I know. I won't be long," she assured him.

He kissed her lightly as he told her, "Good night. I love you."

On that same warm August evening about an hour's drive away in Summerville, Anna and Richard, both now in their early seventies, were coming out of a local movie theater, after seeing *The King's Speech.* They were chatting about how much they enjoyed the film and couldn't understand why they didn't attend the movies more often, when Anna spotted Carolyn and Bud Sanders leaving the theater. She and Carolyn both played guards on their high school basketball team and graduated from High School together in 1957. Anna and Carolyn excitedly hugged each other, because they had not seen each other for more years than they cared to remember. Then, Anna introduced Carolyn and Bud to Richard.

Richard suggested that the couple join them at a pastry shop around the corner, so the ladies could get caught up and the men could get to know one another.

Anna was delighted to discover that Carolyn and Bud in their retirement years had moved to her town less than two miles away. In catching up, they realized that the last time they had seen each other was when Carolyn's sons were in their teens. Anna visited them when she had a booking for a brochure advertising a golf course in their community. Bud laughingly told them that their sons were now forty-seven and fifty-one years old.

At that point, they started discussing their grandchildren. When Carolyn asked Anna how many grandchildren she had, Anna answered, "Nine" at the same time Richard answered, "Eight."

Looking a bit confused Carolyn asked, "Well, which is it?"

A bit annoyed at Richard for excluding Stephanie like he had on other occasions when people asked them how many grandchildren they had, Anna explained, "We have nine grandchildren. Years ago, my oldest son fathered a little girl out of wedlock. Her name is Stephanie. When she was two days old, I got to hold her and tell her hello and good-bye at the same time before she was placed for adoption. She might have been adopted, but she's still my granddaughter wherever she is." She added, "My number one prayer is to live long enough to see her again."

Carolyn was quite moved by Anna's story and encouraged her to not ever give up hope.

The following Friday and Saturday nights, Sadie researched until three or four o'clock in the morning, filling up a legal pad with notes about Bierers from Lancaster County, Pennsylvania to Goleta, California and back to South Carolina. On Sunday night, Sadie was again on her comfortable living room chair with her favorite blanket, using her iPad, taking notes, sipping her favorite Chianti, and nibbling on snacks.

While watching television, Barrett had been observing her out of the corner of his eye. Concerned about the many hours she had spent for the past three days and nights, he got up from his easy chair, joined her and asked, "Are you alright?"

"Oh, I'm fine," she responded confidently. "I know the answers are here somewhere in my iPad. I just have to keep looking."

Barrett told her, "I sure give you credit for perseverance. This is your fourth night at this," and half-jokingly added, "Your research is wearing me out."

Sadie responded, "I think I've found all of Bert's seven children. I've found four men, two women, and one whose name can be male or female. All I need to do is find out which they are and then find out the one that is the middle child.

"How did you find them?" Barrett asked.

"I don't know," she responded. "I just dug deep. If you dig deep enough on the web, you can find almost anything."

"It looks like you're near your finish line," Barrett told her. Then with a pleading look he asked, "How much longer are you staying up? I have to go to bed."

"Just a little while. I'll be there shortly," Sadie responded.

"You've said that for the past three nights and you still didn't come to bed until three or four in the morning. You can't keep doing this to yourself."

"Honey, I'm sorry," she responded. "I'm on a roll. I can't stop now. I have to keep going on this."

Knowing how driven she was, Barrett kissed her gently and told her, "Okay, see you in the morning."

Hours later, actually at exactly two-twenty-five a.m., Sadie exclaimed to herself, "Oh my God! This has got to be my grandmother!"

She grabbed her cell phone and texted Emma, "Hey, I think my grandmother is Anna Weber. If she has a son who was born in 1960, he's my father. I'm so excited." She hit the send button, turned off her iPad, and went to bed.

In the morning, Barrett made coffee. He stuck his head in the hallway and yelled, "Sadie, time to get up. It's six- forty-five." Barrett continued to prepare breakfast.

Sadie wandered in half asleep, "Barrett, I think I found my grandmother. Her name is Anna Weber."

With relief Barrett half-jokingly exclaimed, "Yeah! Now maybe we can finally get some sleep around here." He then added, "What did you find out about her? Where does she live?"

Sadie responded, "I don't know, all I have is her name. If she has a son born in 1960, he would be my father. We'll find him and then maybe he can help me locate my birth mother."

Concerned, Barrett told her, "I sure hope this works out for you. What if they don't want to see you?"

"Their letters said they did," Sadie responded.

Barrett asked her, "What letters?"

Sadie reminded him, "The ones in the file that I got from Social Services."

"But those letters were written over twenty-seven years ago. You don't know what you'll find now," Barrett argued.

"But I have to find out," Sadie said firmly.

With that Barrett asked, "Do you still have the list of counseling services that Social Services gave you with your file?"

Sadie told him that she did and he reminded her that he just wanted to protect her. Sadie had the knowledge that if things did not work out as she had hoped, she would always have Barrett to comfort her.

Later that morning, Emma ran into Sadie's office, with Amy, Debbi, and Diana following right behind her. She excitedly announced, "Sadie, I found him! I found him! I found your birth father!"

Sadie tensed, "Tell me he's an okay guy, not someone whose picture I would find hanging in the post office."

Delighted with her discovery, Emma assured her, "He's A-okay. He's a track coach who sells real estate on the side. His name is Ian McKinney and he lives in Greenville."

"How'd you find him?" Sadie asked.

Emma explained, "It was on a title of real estate. Anna granted some property on Holland Avenue to her son Ian McKinney for the sum of five dollars, love and affection."

"He has a different last name," Sadie observed.

"Yeah," Emma confirmed. "Anna married Richard Weber three years before you were born."

Sadie asked, "What else did you find out about Ian McKinney?"

Emma proudly boasted, "I have his address and his phone number, and he's on Facebook!"

Sadie exclaimed, "Wow! Let's look real quick on Facebook to see what he looks like." They all crowded around Sadie as she pulled up Facebook and saw her birth father for the first time.

"Oh, he's okay, kind of cute," Diana exclaimed, "Great shape for a man old enough to be your father."

"Sadie, why don't you send him a friend request and get to know him, and then you can decide if you want to meet him," suggested Debbi.

Oh, no, no, no, I can't do that," Sadie exclaimed. "What if he hits on me? Oh, that would be so disgusting to have my own father hit on me. It doesn't matter that he wouldn't know who I am. No, I'm not about to send him a friend request."

"Why don't I friend him for you," Amy offered. "I'll let you read all correspondence and then you can determine what kind of a person he is and how you might want to go about meeting him."

"Good idea, do it and keep me informed," Sadie requested. But, she added that in the meantime she wanted to consult their boss, attorney Roger Bledsoe for his professional opinion.

When Sadie asked her boss for his opinion on how she should contact her birth father, he asked her to weigh her options. She did not want to call him on the phone because it was too impersonal. She could find out what his schedule was and arrange a surprise meeting, but didn't want to cause him any possible embarrassment and there was always the possibility of him rejecting her on the spot and she couldn't bear the thought of that happening.

Roger offered to draft a letter to him, saying that he had a client who thinks she's his daughter. That way, it would be his decision whether or not they would meet, and Sadie wouldn't have the risk of either him rejecting her or her causing him any kind of embarrassment. Sadie liked that idea, but asked him to hold off writing the letter until she told her mother what was going on. Her boss agreed.

That same day in early afternoon, Sadie dropped by her mother's house. Her mother was seated in her favorite relaxing place, her front porch swing. Claire could tell by her daughter's walk that something good is going on.

Claire curiously commented, "You look mighty excited. I thought you didn't get off from work until five."

"Roger let me off work early, because I have some exciting news," Sadie explained.

The first thing that flashed through Claire's mind was Sadie might be pregnant. But she was only married for three and a half months and she was on the pill, but it was still a possibility. Rather than guessing, she simply asked, "What's that?"

"I found out who my biological father and grandmother are," Sadie responded excitedly. "My father is Ian McKinney. His age matches the background information Social Services gave you when you adopted me. He's a track coach and sells real estate on the side."

"What about the grandmother who left you all those clues?" asked Claire.

"Her name is Anna Weber. I haven't checked to see..." Sadie didn't get to finish what she was about to say.

Claire interrupted her, "Anna Weber? Good grief, I know exactly who she is and so do you."

Surprised, Sadie asked, "I do? How?"

When we first visited The Millie Lewis Agency, Susan showed us her Wall of Fame. Anna Weber's picture was on it," Claire explained.

"Momma, how am I supposed to remember that?" Sadie questioned. "That was over twelve years ago."

"Later, when Susan hung your picture on the wall, she hung it beside Anna Weber's," reflected Claire. "I remember it as clear as yesterday."

"Oh, my gosh! You have got to be kidding!" Sadie exclaimed excitedly, "We have to let Miss Susan know about this."

Claire removed her cell phone from her pocket and tapped in Susan's number. All she got was Susan's answering machine. "Hello Susan, this is Claire Porter. I've got something important to tell you. You're not going to believe it. Please call me back right away."

Sadie questioned her mother, "Momma, are you sure you're okay with all this?"

Claire reassured her daughter, "Absolutely certain. Honey, I told you we have a bond nothing can break."

Sadie was bursting with emotion, a stronger than ever love for her mother for being so supportive, and the realization that she would soon be meeting her biological family. Before she left to go home and prepare dinner, she made her mother promise to call her as soon as she heard from Susan.

Sadie went home and prepared dinner. Barrett's appetite was as strong as ever, but Sadie's wasn't.

He observed, "You hardly ate a bite of dinner."

"I'm sorry," she responded, feeling really bad because his chopping the onions and peeling the potatoes, was a major part of preparing their meal. "I'm just anxious wondering why Momma hasn't called yet. Maybe she forgot."

"She wouldn't forget something this important," he told her reassuringly.

"I can't stand this waiting for the phone to ring, I've got to call her," Sadie replied impatiently.

She called her mother only to find out that Susan had not returned her call yet. Sadie couldn't wait any longer, she tried to call Susan herself, but she also had to leave a message.

Susan was driving home from work in her Toyota Solaris convertible. The top was up even though it was an extra warm August evening. Earlier she had seen that Claire had left a message, but she planned to return her call after she got home. Her cell phone was chirping again to indicate a new message. She saw that it was Sadie and hit a key to return the call. Sadie answered. Susan asked her, "What's going on? I have two messages here, one from you and one from your mother."

Excitedly, Sadie told her, "Miss Susan, you're not going to believe this. I found my birth grandmother and she modeled for you at your agency. She's Anna Weber."

"What?" exclaimed Susan. Her car swerved. She steadied it and composed herself. "Did you say Anna Weber?"

"Well, I have to confirm a few things. But it looks like she's my grandmother," Sadie responded excitedly.

Susan assured her, "Well, if you confirm that it's her, you couldn't have a sweeter grandmother."

Sadie felt better than ever with the knowledge that her biological grandmother came with a seal of approval from Miss Susan, someone she had admired and respected since she was a little girl. Then a thought came to her, "Maybe you can help me confirm it. I'm absolutely certain my great-grandfather had a daughter named Anna, born around the same time my birth grandmother was born, and that Anna Weber has a son the same age that my birth father would be. It is possible that it is a different Anna Weber, but I'm ninety-nine percent certain it is this Anna Weber."

"What do you want me to do?" Susan offered.

"Maybe you can ask her if her father was Bert Bierer," Sadie requested. "And if she is my grandmother, I don't want to just call her up and say, 'Hello, I'm your granddaughter.' She might not want to see me. If you can find out that she does want to see me, let me know right away."

"Absolutely," exclaimed Susan. "You don't know how special this makes me feel to be a part of something this important."

Susan told her sister-in-law, Lois, who was also her booking agent, Sadie's exciting news. Lois volunteered to call Anna to confirm that her father was indeed Bert Bierer, the veterinarian, poultry pathologist, and author of the book *Indians and Artifacts in the Southeast*. She tried to reach Anna by phone, but was only able to leave a message.

Anna and Richard were on vacation in Manhattan when Lois left the message for her. They returned home to find their answering machine blinking indicating they had several messages. One was from Anna's dentist's office reminding her of her appointment. Another message was from one of Richard's friends wanting to play a round of golf. The third one was from Lois saying, "Hey, Anna, this is Lois. I met someone who thinks they knew your father. Was your father Bert Bierer?"

Anna's father had passed away twenty-four years earlier. Who could Lois be talking about? Her curiosity got the best of her, so she called Lois right away. She confirmed to Lois that Bert Bierer indeed was her father, but when she asked Lois who thought they knew him, Lois replied, "I forgot their name. I'll have to ask Susan and get back to you." She paused and then said, "You know,

Susan and I actually would like for you to go out to lunch with us. We haven't gotten together for some time now."

It was Friday afternoon, so they made arrangements for Anna to stop by the agency at noon the following Monday, and the three of them would ride to lunch together.

On Monday, Anna arrived at The Millie Lewis Agency promptly at noon and Susan and Lois greeted her with hugs. Even though Anna worked out of state a lot, she and Richard had built a lasting friendship with Susan, Lois, and Charlie. Charlie was Susan's husband as well as Lois's brother.

"Anna, before we go to lunch, let me show you the changes we've made since you were last here," invited Susan. Part of the tour included walking Anna through the agency's Wall of Fame. When they passed by the collage of Anna's photographs and magazine advertisements, Anna's vanity took over. She grimaced, knowing that her recent photos and magazine ads were much better. "I need to give you more current pictures," she offered.

They paused again in front of collages of some of their younger talent. One photo was of Sadie when she was sixteen. Susan pointed out other notable talent. "There's Mena Suvari from *American Beauty* and *American Pie*," she boasted.

When they pass by photos of Ashley Scott, Anna couldn't help smiling as she recalled, "Ashley Scott and I got our careers started here the same time over twenty years ago. We trained for the convention together."

Susan pointed out more successful talent. "You know Matt Czuchry from *Gilmore Girls*. And there's Josh Strickland. He's the lead *Tarzan* on Broadway."

When the tour ended, Susan went to her office, while Lois invited Anna to sit in her office. Anna sat across from Lois's desk as Lois started working on her computer with the screen out of sight to Anna.

Susan entered the room carrying a large scrapbook and sat down beside Anna. She opened the scrapbook and told Anna, "I keep pictures of some of my favorite people in this scrapbook," and she started turning the pages.

She showed Anna a photo of Sadie around the age of three. Upon seeing the photo, Anna replied, "Oh, she's cute."

Susan turned some more pages and showed Anna a photo of Sadie when she was an adolescent. Anna said,

"Oh, she's pretty," while she's wondering, why is Susan showing me these pictures? I'm hungry. I skipped breakfast this morning planning on a nice big lunch.

Then Lois turned the computer screen around about ninety degrees and invited Anna to come see the photo on her screen. Anna got up and looked over Lois's shoulder. It was a photo of Sadie in her wedding dress. Anna looked at the screen in total awe, "She is absolutely gorgeous!" she exclaimed and then asked, "Who is she?" as she sat back down beside Susan.

Susan responded, "Remember, how I once told you years ago that I was adopted and how I searched and found my birth family?"

"Yes," responded Anna.

Susan continued, "The girl in the photos that I just showed you and the bride on Lois's screen are all the same. She's adopted too, just like me. She's been searching for her birth parents and has found her grandmother and her grandmother is a model with The Millie Lewis Agency and..."

Susan didn't have to say any more, Anna knew she was talking about her granddaughter Stephanie. She burst into tears, crying uncontrollably. She could not stop crying. It was as if all the tears that she had kept to herself over the past twenty-seven years had come to the surface. Lois handed her a box of tissues. Lois and Susan needed to wipe their tears, too.

When Anna was able to start collecting her thoughts, she told them, "You don't know how I've prayed for this day. I was afraid I wouldn't live long enough to see it happen."

"I walked you through the Wall of Fame thinking that when you saw her picture, you might see some family resemblance and figure out who she was," Susan confessed.

Anna told her, "I've seen her in the faces of thousands of girls over the years."

Susan added, "When she called and said she found her birth grandmother and it was you, I couldn't believe it. Two of my most special people, a little girl grown up and you, her grandmother."

"I was getting worried when I couldn't reach you," Lois told Anna. "When I left a message asking if you were the daughter of Bert Bierer, I was trying to verify for Sadie that you were her grandmother."

Anna asked, "What did you call her?"

Lois responded, "Sadie."

"She was named Stephanie Lynn when she was born," Anna said blowing her nose. "I got to see her and hold her when she was two days old. I put clues in letters to her in her file at the Department of Social Services, hoping that one day she would look for me. She must have figured out who my father was from my clues."

Susan said, "This is some kind of miracle," and then asked Anna if she would like to meet Sadie.

"Are you kidding! Where is she, in the next room?" Anna asked excitedly. The thought flashed through her mind that there might be a hidden camera and this was part of a reality TV show.

"No, she's not here. I can arrange for you to meet her. Are you available tonight?" Susan asked.

"Absolutely!" Anna responded. "When? Where?"

"For now, let's say seven o'clock. I have to check with Sadie first," Susan offered. "If the time suits her, I'll call you to confirm. You can come to my house shortly before seven and I'll take you to meet her. She lives about ten minutes from me."

Anna went to lunch with Susan and Lois, but as hungry as she had been earlier, she ate very little. She was in a daze the whole time. After lunch, they drove Anna back to the agency, where she picked up her car and drove home.

On the drive from the agency to her home, Anna had one major prayer, "Please God help me keep my focus on my driving. I'm so excited about seeing Stephanie, I'm afraid I'll have an accident. Please, get me home safely, then watch over us as Richard drives us to Susan's. Thank you for today, God. Thank you for answering my prayers."

After Anna left the agency, Susan called Sadie at the legal firm where she worked. When she told Sadie that her grandmother wanted to see her, Sadie was delighted to say the least. Seven o'clock was perfect. Sadie immediately buzzed Emma in her office upstairs. Their bosses, who had been one-hundred percent supportive of Sadie's search, shared their excitement and gave them the afternoon off to prepare for the occasion. Their bosses were wise enough to know that Sadie and Emma would be too excited to get any work done anyway.

Sadie called Barrett to tell him that they would be meeting Anna Weber at seven o'clock. She also told him she and Emma were getting off of work early so Emma could do her hair and help her get ready.

Sadie's next call was too tell her mother the big news. Claire immediately offered Sadie her home for the reunion. She and Bryan wanted to meet Anna and Richard too. Claire then called Bryan at his office to tell him what was going on and to ask him to pick up some snacks on the way home from work. She then called Mike to tell him about the reunion. Mike and Sadie's step-mother, Linda, were also interested in meeting Anna and Richard.

Emma dropped Sadie off at her house. After Emma had gone home to pick up her makeup case, Sadie did everything she could to relax. After twenty minutes of yoga, she took a nice, long lavender scented bubble bath while sipping a glass of chardonnay. That helped a little bit, but it wasn't until Emma returned later with her makeup case and hair products to help her get ready and Barrett arrived home from work that she was able to relax a bit more. They were a couple of the most important people in her support system.

When Anna returned home, she had to wait for Richard to come home from playing golf before she could share the good news with him. It was all so surreal. As she was telling him the words of what had transpired earlier at the agency, she could hardly believe what she was saying herself. Richard knowing better than anyone what this meant to Anna, gave her the biggest, longest hug.

She needed to relax and clean up. Her crying session at the agency left her makeup smeared and face puffy. Knowing that you never get a second chance to make a first impression, she wanted to look especially good for her granddaughter. She laid down with chilled sliced cucumbers on her eyes to relieve the puffiness. She tried to take a nap, but was too excited to sleep. She finally gave up and took a long bubble bath with almond bath oil beads and sipped a glass of Riesling. That helped a little bit, but she knew she would not fully relax until she got to see her granddaughter.

CHAPTER 12

God's Thank You

IT WAS A few minutes before seven at Claire's house. Sadie, dressed in a sundress and sandals, nervously kept peeking out of the window in anticipation of her first physical contact with a member of her biological family. Waiting with her were Barrett and both sets of her parents, her mother and step-father, Claire and Bryan, and her father and step-mother, Mike and Linda.

Claire and Bryan's great room was the perfect setting for the reunion. There was plenty of space for all. Sadie's file from Social Services was in a manila envelope on a large dinner table.

When Susan's Toyota Solaris turned into the long driveway, Sadie couldn't wait. She hurriedly left the comforts of air conditioning into the extreme August heat outside, with Barrett and her two sets of parents following her. Barrett and the others stayed behind on the porch and the porch steps as Sadie hurried to meet her grandmother.

Anna climbed out of the convertible leaving Richard and Susan behind. Upon seeing her granddaughter for the first time in over twenty-seven years, the first thought that crossed through her mind was, "This is God's way of saying thank you for stopping the abortion." He had answered her prayers in His way and in His time.

As they ran toward each other with open arms, Anna's first words to Sadie were, "I put in as many clues as I could think of."

Sadie's smiling response was, "And I followed all of them."

After all the introductions had taken place, Claire invited everyone in the house out of the August heat. Once indoors, Anna asked Sadie to call her and Richard, Oma and Opa like all of her other grandchildren did. She explained that was German for grandmother and grandfather. She then reached in her handbag and pulled out the mini-photo album that she had started shortly after Sadie's birth. She gave the album to Sadie telling her, "I saved these photos and newspaper clippings for you in the event you ever came back in my life. This is my way of showing you that you were always loved and never forgotten."

Sadie, most graciously thanked Anna.

The women sat at the table and the men hung out in the kitchen. Sadie described her search from start to finish, explaining how the entire staff at the attorney's office where she worked helped her in her search. She emptied the manila envelope so Anna could see the file.

Anna immediately noticed that some items were missing from Sadie's file. The second and third pages of the first letter that Anna wrote to her were not there, plus the entire letter that Anna wrote to Sadie in 2003 was not there either. She knew that the Department of Social Services had received it, because she still had a letter from them acknowledging they had received it.

After a couple hours of sharing and getting acquainted, Claire asked Anna if she was going to call Ian to tell him about Sadie. Anna tried to call, but she didn't have enough bars for her cell phone to work that far out in the country. Claire offered her cell phone and suggested that Sadie take Anna to their upstairs bedroom to get the best signal and to be able to talk privately. Once upstairs, Anna was immediately able to get Ian on the phone.

Ian was in his pickup truck traveling on I-77 in the middle of nowhere near the North Carolina state line about an hour away from home. He and his twenty-two-year-old son Miles, a senior at the university, were on their way home from acquiring some sporting equipment. The time he answered his phone, his engine quit.

Anna very excitedly told him, "Ian, you'll never guess where I am. I'm at Stephanie's." At the time, she thought she was at Stephanie's home, but later found out it was the home of her mother and step-father.

Ian misunderstood Anna, thinking she said she was at Tiffany's. In the past, Ian had received calls from his mother when she was working out of state. He jumped to the conclusion she was in New York at Tiffany's Department Store. He was extremely upset about his truck dying, plus he was completely worn out from a long day of travel. Trying to stifle his frustration as he pulled his truck off of the highway onto the shoulder, he grumbled, "Mom, now is not a good time. I'm on I-77 and my engine just blew." Fearful he might hang up the phone, she told him, "Ian, I'm with Stephanie. She searched for us and found us."

Ian heard her right that time. Completely forgetting about his immediate predicament on the highway and in total disbelief, Ian asked, "Stephanie? She found us?"

Anna went on to tell him, "Yes, her name's been changed to Sadie. She's right here... standing beside me. She wants to talk to you." Anna handed Sadie the phone, "Here, I'll let you talk to him in private." She then left Sadie alone to talk to Ian, while she went back down stairs to join Susan, Barrett and Sadie's two sets of parents.

It was like music to Ian's ears to hear his daughter's voice for the first time. Her first words to him were, "Hello, Ian."

Ian responded, "Stephanie, I'm sorry. I didn't catch what your name was changed to."

"Sadie," she replied.

"Sadie," Ian said wiping his tears, "you have no idea how much this means to me. This is the answer to my longest running prayer."

Ian and Sadie talked for about twenty minutes. She invited Ian and his fiancée, Grace, to have dinner with her and Barrett on Wednesday.

During the time Ian was talking to her, Miles had gotten out of the truck and sat on the side of the highway. He used his cell phone to call a friend to tow him and his father back home.

After talking to Sadie, Ian joined Miles sitting on the side of the highway. Ian, wiping his eyes, was ecstatic.

Miles questioned him, "What's going on? What was that all about?"

"Miles," Ian reminded him, "Remember when I told you that you have a sister out there somewhere? That was her on the phone. She found us."

Surprised, Miles said, "I don't know what you're talking about."

Ian told him, "Your half-sister, Stephanie. I told you about her."

"Dad," Miles argued, "you never told me I had another sister."

"Are you sure?" Ian questioned.

"I'm absolutely certain. I wouldn't forget something that important," Miles said emphatically.

Ian felt terrible. He didn't know how he could have forgotten to tell Miles about Stephanie. He thought he had made it a point to tell each of his children about her when they were around fifteen years old. He had just told his youngest son Ryan a week ago. With much sincerity Ian apologetically told Miles, "I am so sorry. I thought I told you."

"Well, you didn't," Miles responded feeling a bit left out of something very important.

Ian proceeded to tell Miles about his half-sister. "When I was your age, I fathered a little girl named Stephanie. Her mother and I had broken up, and I didn't find out she was pregnant until your mom and I were engaged to be married. I had to choose between marrying your mom and obtaining my rights to my daughter."

"Wow, that's heavy," remarked Miles with compassion. "So I have another sister, huh?"

"Yeah," Ian told him, "I'll be driving downstate to meet her Wednesday evening. She's invited Grace and me to dinner." He paused and then asked, "When did Matt say he'd be here to tow us home?"

Miles responded, "He should be here soon. I sure hope so. I have an eight o'clock class in the morning and I'm totally exhausted."

It was about midnight when Ian finally arrived home. His eighteen-year-old daughter, McKenna, was still awake studying for her English class at the university. She was curled up on the couch with her laptop computer. When she saw him, she exclaimed, "Daddy, what happened to you? You look like something the cat dragged in."

Ian told her, "The bad news is I've been sitting on the side of I-77 for over an hour. Matt had to come tow us." Then Ian broke down and cried as he told McKenna, "The good news is... remember when I told you that you have a sister out there somewhere? She found us."

With absolute joy, McKenna responded, "Stephanie! She found us? How?"

Ian explained, "It's a long story. Oma called me and put her on the phone. Her name's been changed to Sadie." Wiping his tears he told her, "There's been a hole in my heart ever since I signed that paper."

"Daddy," McKenna said excitedly, "Tell me her full name and I'll look her up on Facebook... She better not be a druggie."

"Her name is Sadie Leigh Chambers," Ian answered.

Ian sat down beside McKenna and looked over her shoulder as she searched for Sadie on Facebook. Ian had only talked to Sadie and had no idea what she looked like. Ian and McKenna cried for joy together when they saw

Sadie for the first time. It was the same picture that Anna saw of Sadie for the first time, the one of her wearing her bridal dress.

"Oh, Daddy, she's beautiful. When can I get to meet her?" she asked.

Ian told McKenna that he and Grace would be driving down to meet Sadie on Wednesday, and he was sure she would be meeting Sadie real soon.

Two days later, an extremely nervous Sadie kept peeking out of her curtains. Barrett was a bit nervous too, although he didn't want to admit it. He didn't want Sadie to be hurt if things didn't work out. For her first meal with her birth father, Sadie planned pizza. She was much too nervous to cook, much less eat.

Sadie's heart must have skipped several beats when she saw a Volkswagen Jetta pull into their driveway. Her heart was racing like crazy when she saw her birth father for the first time. She immediately recognized him from Facebook. A woman also got out of the car. Sadie guessed that the woman, who appeared to be in her late forties, must be Ian's fiancée Grace. Ian had told her that he and his wife Shari, the mother of his four children, had divorced a couple years earlier, after twenty-five years of marriage.

Before Ian had a chance to ring the doorbell, Sadie, followed by Barrett, went out to greet them. Ian and Sadie were both extremely nervous, anxious, and excited. They both cautiously resisted the urge to run into each other's arms. Ian wanted to hold her so tight, but realizing that even though he was her father, he was a stranger to Sadie, and he was afraid he would scare her away. They both wanted to be liked by and accepted by the other.

Holding back his tears, he told Sadie, "I recognize you from your picture on Facebook," and to Barrett, he said, "You must be Barrett." Ian then introduced his daughter and Barrett to his fiancée Grace.

Barrett told him, "Sadie's been nervous all day. Now maybe she'll calm down."

"I feel better already," Sadie assured him, but she was still very nervous.

Ian and Sadie had a most wonderful visit getting to know each other. Neither ate that much. Ian told her, "My truck engine blew the instant my phone rang. I almost didn't answer it... and when Mom said she was with you... well, my feet haven't touched the ground since."

Sadie described how her friends at the law firm helped her in her search and when they looked him up on Facebook, Amy offered to send him a friend request. She said, "Amy told me that after she sent you her personal information, you wouldn't accept her as one of your friends."

Ian asked, "That was your friend? When was that? About a week ago?" Sadie nodded and then he explained to her, "When I first started Facebook, I left it open in the event that one day you might be able to find me on it. I accept most people, but now and then, if someone acts a bit questionable, I turn them down. I remember Amy, she was not interested in track and she wasn't a parent to any of my students. We didn't have any interest in common. I thought she was some young woman hitting on me and

I wasn't interested in being her sugar daddy, so I turned her down."

Sadie continued to tell him in detail about her search and how his letter only had one clue in it, Tara's name. When he told her that he had written his grandparents address in his letter to her, Sadie told him that Social Services had whitened out their address.

When they got on the subject of Tara's letter, which had no clues whatsoever, Sadie asked him if he knew where she was. He told her that Tara had married someone named Doug Barrow, had a son, and moved to a small town outside of Asheville, North Carolina when Doug accepted a job as a forest ranger. The last he had heard, Tara was operating an antique gift shop.

Sadie asked him, "Do you think you could get in touch with her for me and tell her I want to meet her."

Ian told her, "I can tell you where she is."

Sadie was very apprehensive, "No, I don't want to surprise her. She might not want to see me."

Ian tried to assure her, "She will want to see you. I know that without a doubt."

Sadie explained, "I have to be absolutely certain of that. From what I read in my file, she went to a lot of trouble to keep my birth a secret. She might still want it that way."

Ian more firmly told her, "I promise you, she will want to see you."

With concern Sadie said, "I don't want to cause her any embarrassment."

To put Sadie's mind at ease, Ian asked Sadie to give him all of her contact information. He would pass it on to Tara and then it would be left up to Tara to contact her. Feeling comfortable with Ian's idea, Sadie complied by giving him her information.

A little later in the evening, both sets of Sadie's parents dropped by her house, so they could meet Ian and Grace. They were the epitome of Southern Hospitality, inviting them to be a part of Sadie's extended family. By the time Ian left, he and Sadie both felt comfortable enough to embrace each other like they wanted to when they first met several hours earlier.

Several days later, in a small town outside of Asheville, North Carolina, Tara Barrow arrived at her antique store. She always arrived about fifteen minutes prior to opening, so she would have time to check her emails. This morning was no different than all the others for more than two decades, that was until she checked her inbox and saw an email from Ian McKinney. What did he want? She had not had any contact with him since that afternoon in June 1983, when he called her asking if she was absolutely certain that she wanted to put their little Stephanie up for adoption. She recalled that it was not something she wanted to do, but something she had to do. She had no choice. She remembered crying non-stop for weeks. She started to hit the delete button. That was a part of her life she thought she had put behind her forever. She didn't want to go there. But something made her open it. She almost collapsed when she read, "Tara, Stephanie found us. She wants to see you. Her name was changed to Sadie. Her contact information is attached. Best regards, Ian." Tara's knees buckled as she said, "Oh my God. My little angel."

A week had passed since Sadie met her biological father and grandmother. Her anxiety was getting the best of her, because she had not heard from her biological mother. Claire picked up on her daughter's restlessness and invited her out to lunch to a nice restaurant with a Cajun cuisine.

"I needed to get out of the house," Sadie said, "I have to think about something else besides wondering if Tara's going to call."

"It's only been a week," Claire said assuredly, "Think positive. She could be out of town like Anna was."

When the waiter took their order, Claire didn't hesitate to order their signature meal, shrimp etouffee. But Sadie, with little appetite, asked for their house salad, wondering if she would even be able to eat that.

While waiting for their food, Claire tried to engage her daughter in positive conversation. She suggested they invite Anna and Richard to campmeeting in October, as that would be a great way for them to meet some of their extended family. Sadie and her mother were engaging in small talk, when Sadie's cell phone chirped indicating she had received a text message.

She immediately came alive. "Oh my God! It's a text from Tara. She says she's sorry for not getting in touch earlier. She's happy, but overwhelmed. She needed time for it to process and to tell her son. She wants to meet me and wants her sister Nicole to be with her when she meets me."

Labor Day that year was the most special of all Labor Days in Anna's seventy-plus years of living. She arranged for Sadie and Barrett to meet with Ian and three of his other children, Miles, McKenna, and Ryan at her and

Richard's home. Most of their time was spent taking pictures. Ian's other son John couldn't attend, because of medical problems his little girl, Mary Jane, was having, but he got to meet Sadie later.

About a week later, the day had finally arrived for Sadie to meet her birth mother. Through texting, Sadie invited Tara and her sister Nicole to have dinner at her house.

Sadie wanted to look her very best. Her dear friend Emma volunteered to do her hair again. When Emma arrived, she placed her handbag on the floor beside the couch partially out of view.

Barrett was doing everything possible to make this the perfect setting for Sadie and Tara to meet. Besides helping tidy up their home, he planned to serve them dinner, so they could relax and get to know each other. His main role, however, was to be supportive to Sadie who was more nervous than she had been before meeting Anna and Ian lumped together.

Emma's role was more than just doing Sadie's hair. She was there for support too. Their bosses at the law firm where they worked, for the third time in two weeks, gave them both the afternoon off to prepare for a special occasion. After Emma finished doing Sadie's hair, she graciously left Sadie and Barrett alone to meet Tara.

Sadie and Barrett were both peeking out of the window when a car pulled into their driveway. It was Tara and her sister, Nicole. Sadie was very nervous and apprehensive. She didn't want to wait for the doorbell. With Barrett right behind her, she walked out to meet her birth mother who was equally nervous and apprehensive.

Tara had her own fears, too, with her main fear being that Sadie might hold it against her for putting her up for adoption. She wanted to be accepted by Sadie just as much as Sadie wanted to be accepted by her. They both resisted the urge to run into each other's arms, but they did hug for a while.

The love, warmth, and sincerity of both of the women dominated their reunion. Barrett served dinner, while the three ladies got acquainted. Tara apologized for taking so long to get in touch with her. She explained, "It took me a while to collect my thoughts. Nicole was the only person I could ever talk to about you and she was out of town."

Nicole said, "If I had known, I would have come home sooner"

Tara added, "It took me a while to muster up the courage to tell my husband. He wasn't too happy about the situation."

"But once he meets you, he'll come around," Nicole said to put Sadie's mind at ease.

"The hardest part was telling my son Kenneth," shared Tara. She was in the process of telling Sadie about her son, when their conversation was interrupted by the ringing of their door bell. Barrett answered it to see Emma standing there looking very embarrassed.

Emma apologetically told him, "I forgot my pocketbook." Barrett invited her in and brought Emma to join the others.

As Sadie smiled, wondering if Emma's curiosity might have gotten the best of her, she introduced Emma, "Tara, Nicole, I would love for you to meet Emma. She was my main super sleuth who helped me find you. Emma, this is Tara and this is her sister Nicole."

"I'm pleased to meet both of you," Emma said bubbling with excitement.

They invited Emma to stay and visit for a while, but she turned them down. Before leaving, she retrieved her pocketbook which was still on the floor by the couch.

Sadie, Barrett, Tara, and Nicole continued with what had to be one of the most memorable and special days of all their lives.

Epilogue

On June 21, 2011, Ian and Anna celebrated Sadie's 'first' birthday with her. Ian drove from Greenville and Anna drove up from Summerville to meet Sadie at a restaurant near her job at the law firm. They both wanted to give her something extra special to make up for all of the birthdays they couldn't celebrate with her.

Anna gave her an antique amethyst necklace with a sterling silver chain that had been her Aunt Mary's. Ian gave her a beautifully sculptured crystal vase that had been passed down to him from his great-grand-mother via his grandmother.

Claire invited Anna to spend the better part of a day with her, including lunch, to share Sadie's growing up years through report cards, pictures, videos, and newspaper articles.

Tara arranged for Sadie and Claire to join her, her sister Nicole, and her mother Andrea Harper for a weekend of getting acquainted with each other in the mountains. Claire brought photographs and videos of Sadie as she was growing up to share with Tara, Nicole, and Andrea. At a later date, they included their husbands and Tara's son.

After Anna and her granddaughter were reunited, Anna wanted to mail a copy of the photograph of Sadie in her wedding gown to Dr. Brantley Holcomb, the abortion doctor, so he could see the life that he had almost taken. She found out that he had died several years earlier.

Three years later, in Grandmomma's den a baby shower was held for Sadie. Among the many guests were Anna, Andrea, Tara, and Nicole.

Anna, Ian, and Tara continue to stay in touch with Stephanie on a regular basis.

The two missing pages from Anna's first letter and the entire letter that she wrote to Stephanie in 2003 are still missing from the files of the Department of Social Services.

Facts And Coincidences

In 1996, Susan and her husband Charlie hosted a very large Christmas party. Among their special guests were Anna and Richard, who watched a small group of young teenagers line dancing, not realizing that one of them was Stephanie.

Claire and Mike Ayers named their pontoon boat after their adopted daughter SADIE LEIGH.

Claire and Mike Ayers sold the SADIE LEIGH to their close friends Donnie and Patricia Adams.

Donnie Adams was a cousin to Ian's wife, Shari.

Donnie Adams' family took Ian's family boating on the SADIE LEIGH.

When Social Services called Claire to pick up their baby, it was Donnie's wife, Patricia, who took the phone call in the dentist office.

Donnie's son, Joshua, grew up with and went to school with Sadie.

When the train hit Sadie, it was Donnie's son, Joshua, who found her on the side of the road and came to her aid.

Ian's brother Martin was a member of the same Rotary Club as Sadie's step-father Bryan Porter. They were actually chatting together prior to a Rotary Meeting on August 30th, at the exact time that Anna was being told by Susan that her granddaughter had found her and wanted to meet her.

Adoption Searches

When you first start your search, research the laws for the state where your adoption was finalized. Check with your state's social services department or one of the national organizations listed below, because the laws are constantly changing. The laws pertaining to the registries that are government maintained vary from state to state. Place your search with free confidential registries. There are some very good private registries that do wonderful work. If you decide to pay for an adoption searcher/investigator that is not associated with the state and is independent, never pay up front for your search and always work with a no find-no fee guarantee

You might need to sign on more than one registry. For example, the Department of Social Services' Adoption Reunion Registry in my state of South Carolina can only allow people to sign their registry if DSS handled the adoption. Plus, state law excludes grandparents from signing their registry. However, anyone who has a South Carolina adoption connection can use the South Carolina Adoption Reunion Registry, thus, they allow grandparents to sign their registry. I only recently discovered that this registry existed.

Keep a list of where you have placed your information and after you have been reunited, please go back and let them know they can remove your search post.

If you have any questions at all that you have found/ reunited with the person you so desperately wanted to find, don't hesitate to do a DNA test to confirm. They are reasonably priced and will give you the satisfaction that your search is over.

There are a number of good registries out there. Here are a few registries and organizations to consider. They don't ask for money up front.

Adoption Search Groups

Florence Crittenton Home Adoption Reunion Registry *www.FlorenceCrittentonHome.com*
At one time, there were over two-hundred Florence Crittendon Homes for unwed mothers. They were in most states across the nation, plus a few were overseas. Twenty-seven of these homes are still in operation today.

International Soundex Reunion Registry – is American based *http://www.isrr.org/index.htm*

South Carolina Adoption Reunion Registry *www. SouthCarolinaAdoptions.com*

Kentucky Adoption Reunion Registry *www.KyAdoptions.com*

Florida Adoption Reunion Registry – FARR *http://www. adoptflorida.com/Reunion-Registry.htm*

National Organizations

Two main national organizations that do not have adoption reunion registries, but can put you in touch with a representative of your state who can help you are:

American Adoption Congress - AAC *www.americanadoptioncongress.com*
P O Box 42730
Washington, DC 20015

Concerned United Birth Parents - CUB *www.cubirthparents.org*
P O Box 341442
Los Angeles, CA 90034-9442

The above information was provided by the South Carolina Adoption Reunion Registry.

64400798R00094

Made in the USA
Lexington, KY
06 June 2017